Valeria

The Ventura Series

First Edition

C.A.Watts

Published in 2021 by
Ballads & Bards Bookhouse

Ballads & Bards Bookhouse
Wonnarua Country
Suite 92, Ground Floor
1 Market Street,
Newcastle, NSW 2300
AUSTRALIA
www.balladsandbardsbookhouse.com

A catalogue record of this work is available from the National Library of Australia

Valeria: The Ventura Series
ISBN: 978 0 6451408 0 4 (paperback)

10 9 8 7 6 5 4 3 2 1

Cover Design
Kozakura

Map Illustrator
Jamie Hall

Portrait Illustrator
Lirak Lila

Text Design
Istvan Szabo

Editor
Dr Danny Decillis

Printed by Ingram Spark, a Lightning Source company, Kindle Direct Printing, an Amazon company, and Draft2Digital.

Ballads & Bards Bookhouse acknowledges the Traditional Owners of the country on which we work, the Wonnarua and Awabakal nations, and recognises their continuing connection to their land, waters and culture. We pay respects to their Elders past, present and emerging.

*Dedicated to Jodie,
who housed me while I first wrote this,
who was by my side when the idea first came to me,
who has been a steadfast and unwavering friend all
these years.*

Table of Contents

CHAPTER 1

The Family Royce

§§

This isn't the beginning of the story. This is simply where it gets interesting, where my sister and I come in.

Ventura wasn't unknown to us. It was centuries of our family history. We knew it was there. We knew who owned it. We knew it was worth a lot. We knew that it could never be sold… and we knew that every generation it was passed down when the old owner died. Never, even in our wildest dreams, did we ever think it would be passed down to us.

"Your grandmother loved you two," our father had stated like that was all there was to it. Richard Royce was a tall and bulky man, with a shaved head and a long greying moustache and goatee that fell to the centre of his chest. His eyes were almost black, but they glittered with kindness. Never was there a raised voice or hurtful tone. We were lucky to have him for a Dad and we made a point of showing him we knew it.

1

Of course, we knew Grandma loved us; we were her grandkids, but she had a lot of grandkids and a lot of kids for that matter. Why us? What made us so special? We were certainly grateful, but it didn't seem to make sense and first and foremost, I was always the inquisitive type.

"It was her that gave you your nicknames, remember?" Dad had gone on, while we sat staring at the letter from Grandma's lawyer that was to alter our lives forever.

In my entire living memory we'd only ever been Rogue and Ranger; never Rivven and Raven. Not even our school used our birth names and no, I hadn't remembered. But when I thought about it, that was right. She had given us our nicknames, but that just led to me questioning even more things that weren't adding up.

I'd been named after my many times great grandmother Raven, who was alive when Ventura was being designed and built. Ventura was my grandmother's pride and joy, a testament to her family legacy and her entire heritage. If anything, she'd want me to feel that same pride due to my namesake… but she wanted to call me something else. Why? Why Rogue and Ranger? And why leave Ventura to us when she still had living children?

Yes, we were the first set of twins born to the family since Raphael and Romana. It was Raphael who was married to Raven when construction on Ventura first began, and it was the twins' father Romira who had originally orchestrated the build, but centuries had passed since then.

After they died in a tragic fire, Romana was given ownership of Ventura and when she died, it was handed down to Rachel, Raphael and Raven's daughter who Romana had cared for after they died. It had been passed down ever since… and now it was ours, but why?

It had never before been passed down by more than a single generation and Grandma Reina was an absolute stickler for tradition. None of it made sense, but I was considered paranoid by my family to question it so thoroughly.

"Why does it bother you so much not to know?" my mother Lyla had asked us. Mum was a tiny woman. Rogue and I were both taller than her by the time we were twelve. She had hair that sat just below her shoulders and was never the same colour two months in a row, and cool green eyes that reminded you of still, quiet water. She wore angled glasses with a black frame most of the time and was usually wearing an apron covered in either flour or paint, depending on her hobby preference that week.

At that moment, it was like she'd never met me. When your family has something that is so large and is worth so much, and it ends up being left in a will to two kids, teenagers or not, you're going to wonder why, especially when questioning everything- from why is the sky blue to why do square roots exist- had been my default setting my entire life. What I didn't understand was why my parents didn't wonder why.

"I guess they just understood Grandma Reina better than we did," my sister had whispered to me on the way back to our room. Even though we weren't children and there were plenty of rooms for us to have one each, we still shared the one. When our parents asked us whether we wanted our own rooms, all they got in reply was a dumb look. It had never occurred to us that we could be separated, let alone want to be.

My sister plopped down onto her bed, but I walked over to the dresser. There, stuck into the side of the mirror was a series of photos. Us growing up; our parents bringing us home as babies; Grandma Reina with her husband, Grandpa Lee, who had taken the Royce name for Grandma, as she was the last of her line, and only a man of such dignity and respect would have been a match for her; all of us on the family grounds last Christmas; and finally, one with great however many times grandma Rachel, all of five years old, standing beside Romana after the death of her parents had left her orphaned.

I locked eyes with myself in the mirror. Raven Royce. Ranger. I was shorter, slighter, and paler than my sister. Rogue was almost so tall she had to bob down to see her whole face. My large eyes were a bright blue, sitting on either side of a pointy nose on a round oval face. Dirty blonde hair fell over my broad shoulders and down almost to my hips in a sleek straight sheet. Moles and freckles were splattered across my body from my large forehead down, and as I gazed into my eyes, wishing my lashes were thicker, I had to raise myself onto my tiptoes to get close enough.

I eventually gave up trying to find the answer in the mirror and turned to face my sister. Rogue was a solid half a foot taller than me, and her olive skin always tanned where mine burned, which led to far more freckles. Her face was longer, her hair was a dark brown and her eyes were an icy blue that felt like they pierced your soul.

Dad, ever the Dungeons and Dragons nerd, always said we matched our nicknames perfectly: me; smaller, swifter, and built for ranged weapons and Rogue; tougher, a deadly hand, and a near silent mover. She could get to the kitchen at two in the morning and heat leftovers without our parents ever hearing a peep. Regardless, I found just as many answers looking at her as I did staring at myself… none.

I sat down next to her and from her place, sprawled across the centre of the bed on her stomach, she groaned: "Move, there's no room."

"You have a queen size bed," I snorted derisively.

"Exactly. It's at capacity," her muffled voice drifted out from underneath the pillow.

"Ha HA," I responded sarcastically. "Your wit knows no bounds."

"Witty enough to inherit the family estate, apparently," she shot back, still into her pillow.

Yes… but WHY?

§

The day the letter came, four days before, Rogue and I were at school. "She's done it again!" our friend Gia hissed to me as she planted herself on the bus seat beside me. Gia was brown all over. She had tanned skin the colour of an iced coffee and small, bright brown eyes with lashes that seemed to go on forever. Her almost black hair fell just past the shoulders in kinks and waves. She was the tallest girl in our year and there were times when certain people gave her a hard time. Mainly, a girl named Reina, who enjoyed a lot of names that really hurt Gia.

Reina was the type who considered herself perfect; perfect skin, perfect hair, perfect height, perfect life. So, if your family had less money, you were trash; if your family had more money, then you were pretentious and entitled. If you straightened your hair, you were a try hard, but if you left it natural, you weren't 'taking care of yourself'. There was no way to win against her and so there were many who took the: 'if you can't beat them, join them' stance. As such, she had amassed a crowd of followers who all acted like her.

Gia didn't know her relatives. She struggled with dyslexia and fought for every academic achievement she had. That was how we met. When she moved to town with her foster family she was placed into the same school support program I was in for my ADHD. She never wore makeup, and her height could have put the Harlem Globetrotters to shame. This all made her a wonderfully placed target for Reina and her groupies. Her family, her height, her dyslexia, her skin tone; because "that colour shirt really doesn't suit you, sweetie"; all of it made Gia the perfect prey.

The worst part of it was the fact that Reina just so happened to be our cousin, named after our grandmother. Because of this, we weren't able to set her straight or we'd cop it once we got home, because of course "Reina is a beautiful, smart girl! She's kind to everyone!" her mother, our Aunty Regina, would say. If she caught wind of us speaking out against her daughter, she'd take her outrage out on her husband, Uncle Reiner, who would, in turn, take it to Dad, his brother.

Even though Dad was well aware that Reina had some deceptive, shady tendencies, he was most definitely a 'stay in your own lane' type of man and if there was one thing he expected in his life above all else, it was peace. That was part of the reason he didn't really care that he'd been overlooked with the inheritance of Ventura. If it wasn't his, the drama surrounding it wasn't either.

Rogue and I didn't care whether or not Reina was beautiful, smart, or our cousin; we hated her with every fibre of our being. It made things worse that not only was she our age; she was at our school and in our classes too. Rogue responded in a far more mature and adult manner. She kept the peace, spoke calmly and respectfully, no matter how Reina was behaving and refused to be drawn in, much like our father, to the drama that followed Reina around. I, however, had a completely different tack. I was the impulsive one who responded on instinct and acted before thinking. I was the protector who would gladly throw away my reputation to go to bat for someone who was being unfairly targeted. I was the one Rogue had spent most of her life keeping in check to stop me from going too far and getting into trouble.

"Don't worry. Aunty Regina and Uncle Reiner are sending her to a private school so come the end of the year, you'll probably never see her again," Rogue pointed out.

"And when you have events she's invited to?" Gia pressed, raising an eyebrow.

"Gotta have them to worry about her being invited to them," I retorted. My father was not the most social of people, especially with the extended family. Mum, Rogue and I were all he wanted. We hadn't even been to a family function since the funeral we had for Aunty Rhiannon, Dad's sister. She disappeared years ago and still, no one knows what happened to her.

"She's such a pain," Rogue cut in factually. "She's giving the family a bad name."

"Freedom… not bad," Gia smiled, ignoring her, nodding and displaying a row of straight, white teeth as she pictured it.

"Wait what about you?" she asked, the smile dropping off her face.

"Ha!" Rogue snorted with laughter. "Mum and Dad said they were thinking about sending us too… before Ranger lost it." She raised an eyebrow in a 'go on', motion.

"I wouldn't call getting on my hands and knees and screaming losing it," I sighed, breathing out slowly. "There was begging among the screams, you just couldn't hear them."

"We weren't about to let them stick us with Reina until we finished school. We almost died when we were told she was going to start with us," Rogue said. "And there was no reason to change this late. We started here; we'll finish here."

Ten minutes later, we were off the bus and at our front door. The second we'd gone through it Mum was upon us, bawling her eyes out. "Mum! What's wrong?" Rogue called over her tears. She took a shuddered breath, before leading us into the lounge room, where our father was seated in his favourite armchair. When we walked into the room, he looked up and we saw that his face, too, was tear stained. He beckoned us over. We sat down on the arms of his chair and he put an arm around each of us.

"What is it, Dad?" I asked flatly. And so we found out that Grandma Reina had died, and Ventura… was ours.

CHAPTER 2
Inheritance

§§

Dad handed us an official looking letter on fancy stationery, with signatures and stamps at the bottom. As I read it through slowly, Rogue read over my shoulder.

To Mr and Mrs Richard Royce

This letter is to hereby inform Richard and Lyla Royce of the Last Will and Testament of Reina Alexandria Royce. I, Gerard Bentley, Mrs Royce's attorney, have been charged with the responsibility of executing this, her Last Will and Testament, with each benefactor being individually informed of their entitlements.

To Mr Richard Royce, Mrs Royce leaves her antique automobile models, once belonging to her late husband, your father, Mr Lee Royce, to do with what you wish.

To Mrs Lyla Royce, Mrs Royce leaves the family tapestries, which are not to be sold and must remain within the property known legally as Ventura Estate and Grounds.

To Miss Rivven and Raven Royce, Mrs Royce leaves Ventura Estate in its entirety, never to be sold, and it is her dearest wish for you to reside there.

To the Royce family, Mrs Royce leaves a piece of advice: The light need not be bright, to shine through the darkest night.

My condolences to your family for your loss, and if you have any questions, do not hesitate to contact me. I will arrive on the 24th of November to escort you to the estate.

In regards, with deepest sympathy, Gerard Bentley
Attorney for Mrs Reina Alexandria Royce

The letter was left on the lounge room coffee table after that. Nobody really wanted to look at it. We weren't sure whether to believe it, but when Dad called Uncle Reiner, we learned it was no practical joke. Grandma Reina had passed, and Rogue and I were to inherit Ventura.

"I didn't even know she was sick," Rogue breathed sullenly, up in our bedroom.

"Us? Us?" I had spat. "Why would she leave it to us?"

"Maybe she thought we could take care of it the best."

"No, she would've given it to Dad or Uncle Reiner if she just wanted it looked after. We're kids."

"Whatever the reason is, we'll most likely find out when we get there," Rogue sighed.

Neither of us cried. Neither of us could. It's not that we weren't sad or upset that we'd lost our grandmother, or that we thought being given an estate made up for losing her, but to be so young and have such a large responsibility dropped onto you; where you've got no choice but to take it and make sure you do a good job, and nobody knows why the job was given to you in the first place, it becomes really hard to have one emotion long enough for each one to affect you. All we could do… was think.

§

We'd been waiting for two hours already, but the lawyer still hadn't shown up. It was the 24th of November and two in the afternoon. Dad had gotten a phone call the night before telling us to be ready by noon.

"The wait is making me so anxious; I'm going to give myself a rash," I muttered.

While we were waiting, Dad had received another call, this one from Uncle Reiner. He was so mad that we were able to hear the conversation through the phone from the other side of the house. He wasn't happy that Rogue and I had been given Ventura and all Reina had been given was money. We all knew that if Reina was given Ventura, Uncle Reiner would've had the whole estate bulldozed and built hotels on it. He never would have respected his mother's wishes, which was exactly what Dad pointed out. That didn't change the fact that Uncle Reiner had officially contested the will in an attempt to get around what Grandma wanted and seize the estate.

By the end of that phone call, everybody in the house had a headache. Dad had always been a calm and composed man; never getting irritable or agitated; forever dignified and magnanimous. This was the first time we'd ever experienced him like this. He was outraged. "HE KNOWS THAT MUM WOULD HAVE THOUGHT THIS DECISION THROUGH! WHO DOES HE THINK HE IS TRYING TO OPPOSE HER WILL? IF THE GIRLS WEREN'T THE BEST PEOPLE FOR THE ESTATE, THEY WOULDN'T HAVE BEEN CHOSEN!" we all heard Dad bellowing to Mum from the kitchen.

I sighed. Rogue sat there, frozen. She didn't like hearing Dad yell. The doorbell rang. I sighed again and got up to answer it. It was the lawyer.

"Are we ready?" he asked, smiling grandly. He was a pale, fat man with a balding head and one crooked tooth. His eyes were small, and he squinted through black, round glasses. I would have shivered just looking at him, but that probably would have offended him.

"Only for two hours!" Dad yelled, coming in from the kitchen. "Where the bloody hell have you been?"

"Held up at the office, my good man! Shall we be off?!" he smiled again.

We both looked at Dad, not sure what to do. As soon as he met our eyes, he seemed to deflate, and his face lost its redness. "Let's go girls," he sighed wearily. Rogue and I grabbed our suitcases and followed Dad out of the house.

§

The Ricadonna Hotel was the closest hotel to Ventura with a vacancy. It had a grey polished stone façade with roman style columns and a wide expanse of open grass out the front on either side of a long, wide driveway. The foyer was a monstrous cathedral with the roof so far away, you couldn't even make out the design on the ceiling. We'd be here until the key was delivered at nine o'clock Monday when the local lawyer's office opened. It was part of the will that no spare keys were kept, and the original could only cross from hand to hand; no couriers and no mailing allowed.

"Couldn't you at least have sprung for five stars?" a deep voice drawled behind us, as we stood in the check in line. We turned and found Uncle Reiner sitting at a café style table, reading a newspaper and sipping an espresso, one foot resting on the opposite knee. He was over six feet tall, with pale skin and a freshly shaven face. He had straw brown hair with scattered greys throughout that was slicked back with some sort of product. The picture of 'image is everything', he was wearing a grey three piece suit with shiny black shoes and a matching belt. The look of disgust on his face changed to a smug smirk at the fact that he'd figured out where we were going, managed to get here first without us knowing, and then surprised us on our arrival.

My head snapped to Dad so fast I got whiplash. He seemed eerily calm. "If you think it's beneath you, you could always leave. Four and a half, I think, is plenty, Reiner."

"You would," he retorted superiorly.

"How are Regina and the kids, Reiner?" Mum piped up in an attempt to head off the inevitable fight.

"Very tired. They're up in our suite," he responded with a smile. "Regina is very excited to show you her latest imports. We just returned from Europe!" he announced with emphasis. "Shall we arrange dinner for tonight?"

"Oh, ok!" Mum started, looking from Reiner to Dad and back again. Dad gave a 'if we have to' shrug and shake of his head, and so Mum said "yes, of course!"

"Wonderful! We'll see you in the restaurant at six," Uncle Reiner responded, folding up his paper and getting to his feet.

"Greeeeeat," I groaned in a low long sigh until Rogue nudged me. "Great!"

§

It was not great. It was cold and tense, and uncomfortable. Our cousins weren't there: "Jetlag! Poor dears, they're so tired!" It was filled with Aunty Regina fawning over her new handbag and matching shoes while Mum smiled kindly, ever politely puzzled at how obsessed she was with her designer wear.

Mum was a practical woman. If her shoes didn't have holes in them, then the ones she had were fine, but she was always supportive of any interest her loved ones had and family was family.

Aunty Regina was sightly taller than Uncle Reiner, exaggerated by her high heel collection, with golden blonde hair that fell to her shoulders and deep, brown eyes. Her skin was light and freckled, but her face was a plain tan due to the thickness of her makeup.

As the entrée was being served, Uncle Reiner turned the conversation. "I really don't know what to do with Mother gone."

"I would assume very much the same as what you've been doing the past several years, Reiner," Dad responded, holding up no pretence.

"It's not the same without knowing she's going to be where we always found her," he said, shaking his head. "And with things as they are, I'm not confident of Ventura's future."

"Not this again," Dad groaned. "Girls, would you like to eat dinner by the pool?"

"Yes," I jumped up faster than a jack in the box.

"Very much so," Rogue said at the same time. Before our Uncle even had the chance to protest, we were out of our chairs and halfway across the restaurant. "That was close," she whispered, glancing back anxiously.

"You're telling me. What are the odds on an all out brawl when Uncle Reiner brings up eldest inheritance rights again?" I asked.

"Better than the lottery," Rogue responded drily. We'd reached the hallway before we heard the first shouts coming from the restaurant.

"Run," I ordered, breaking into a sprint. We both took off up the stairs, not willing to wait for the elevator, our uncle and Dad's shouts following us as we ran.

CHAPTER 3
The Ricadonna

§§

After a restless night, Rogue and I woke to an unpleasant surprise: a blonde haired, blue eyed boy of twelve, with a pale complexion and a look of contempt on his face barely half a metre from my nose.

"What do you want, Rowan?" I grumbled, sitting up. Reina's little brother, Rowan; and if he was here, she wasn't far away. Rowan continued to stare.

"Get out, runt!" Rogue hissed, jumping out of bed and stomping over to him. Rowan screamed and ran from the room. "How did he get in here?" she growled.

"I don't know. Maybe he stole a key from housekeeping," I groaned, getting out of bed. "But that means Reina's sneaking around too." Rogue and I exchanged a dark look.

After quickly dressing, we went down to the hotel restaurant and found our parents. "Surprised they let you back in Dad," I joked. I sat down edgily, not sure what to expect.

"Hello girls!" Mum greeted us with a forced smile and an all too cheery voice.

"Mum," Rogue nodded, sliding into a chair beside me. "Dad."

"What are we talking about?" I asked, looking around the table.

"Well, isn't it obvious?" a highly obnoxious voice cut in. The ice fell off her tongue and went right down my spine with a shudder. That voice was worse than screws in a blender; Reina.

She and her parents walked around the table, taking seats on the other side. She came into view as she took a place in between her mother and the spare seat next to Rogue, which was to be filled by Rowan not a minute later. Uncle Reiner had a hard look on his face, avoiding eye contact, while Aunty Regina gave a dazzling smile as she sat down with a flourish, clearly committed to pretending the events of the previous night's dinner had never happened.

Reina looked exactly like Rowan. She had curly blonde hair, and icy blue eyes exactly like Rogue's, except that hers were cold; calculating.

"What, Reina?" Rogue snapped. It wasn't like Rogue to be snippy. The stress of the situation was obviously starting to get to her.

"Isn't it obvious?" she repeated, with an air of superiority. "They're talking about what's going to happen with Ventura."

"There's no need to discuss it, considering none of you own it," Rogue reminded them, sitting back in her chair. "We do."

"Well, obviously that's not possible, due to the fact that you are teenagers and cannot possibly take care of an estate. It's highly inappropriate," Uncle Reiner said. I raised an eyebrow.

"Well, it's a good thing that isn't your decision to make," Dad cut in. "No one can change what has happened and no one can change Mother's decision. Rogue and Ranger have the deed and their names have been signed to it. No other names can be added until the both of them have died and Ventura has been passed down." The fluency of Dad's lie was impressive. We hadn't even *seen* the deed yet.

Uncle Reiner looked mutinous and even Aunty Regina's false smile fell from her face for just a split second.

"YOU HAVE THE DEED?" Reina squealed. "How can you? It's always kept in Ventura! It's not supposed to be taken out! BUT THAT'S NOT *FAIR!* I was named after Grandma! Ventura is supposed to be MINE!"

"That's enough!" Mum hissed, looking around for the security she expected to be watching them after last night. "Sit down!"

"Yes, Reina; do," Aunty Regina agreed, fanning herself with a hand. "You're embarrassing yourself."

"But-" she began again.

"~Sit!" her father growled. Reina immediately sat down, but Rogue and I stood up.

Something had happened since we'd taken our seats; a look from Rogue that asked a very specific question, and a subtle nod from me in return as an answer. No more wondering. We didn't know why this had happened, but it had, and teenagers or not, we needed to step up to the responsibility Grandma had left us. Now was the time to claim it, and make it clear we would fight for it if necessary.

"Reina, perhaps Ventura was meant to be yours. If you think~," I began, turning to Uncle Reiner and Aunty Regina. "~that naming your daughter after the owner and sucking up at every moment possible was you earning the right to Ventura, then yes, it is meant to be hers. But, clearly, you wasted your time trying to win over Grandma Reina. She knew that if she gave it to you or your family, it would be gone, and if she gave it to my parents, Dad would feel honour bound to give you a share. Well, we don't. Ventura was built for our family and you will not destroy centuries of work and love for that estate by throwing some money at a lawyer to get your hands on it!" I stared around at the table and when nobody spoke, I turned and walked away with Rogue at my heels.

"How do we get our hands on the deed?" Rogue asked quietly. "That was a real Hail Mary Pass. Thanks, Dad. Now we have to do it as soon as we can before they try to do the dirty and get one of their names on it."

"Blondie said it's kept in the estate, and in the will, it didn't say we were being given the deed. I'm guessing that means we need to find it ourselves. The whole family needs to go there to get what was promised them in the will. I'm guessing it's the same for us," I told her.

"But that wouldn't be smart, because someone could get there first and sign their names to the deed before the actual chosen people got there," she pointed out. "Does Grandma's will overrule the estate's deed?"

"We're the only ones with the key. The rest of the family that gets there before we do gets rooms in town until our arrival. But…" I drifted off. A gut wrenching feeling had just crept into me.

"What?" Rogue asked in almost a whisper.

"The lawyer has the key…" I began, concerned. "And it's obvious that he was the one who told Uncle Reiner where we were going. If Uncle Reiner has been paying this lawyer off, maybe he already has the key…" I finished.

"That could get him arrested! And the lawyer would be disbarred and charged with fraud or something! That lawyer's more the kind of person who would string him along to get the most out of him, then run," Rogue said thoughtfully, analysing the situation. "Plus, there's more than one lawyer at the firm. This lawyer won't get his hands on the key until the office opens in the morning. So, until nine o'clock tomorrow at least… it's safe," she concluded.

"Ok, he doesn't have it, but he will by morning if we don't do something now… and Ventura is ours… so if we ask for it, he can't refuse," I gave a single nod. "Let's go find him."

At the front desk of the hotel, we found a frazzled looking woman. "We need the room number for Gerard Bentley," I ordered. "He's the lawyer escorting us to our estate and we need to speak with him."

"Names?" she sighed.

"Rivven and Raven Royce," Rogue said.

"Oh!" she gasped, her glasses sliding down her nose. She quickly readjusted them. "Well, I can't give out private information, but I can call up and let him know you want to see him?" She dialled the phone and after a few rings, the lawyer picked up.

"Who is it?" his gruff voice resounded from the earpiece.

"Hello, Mr Bentley? This is Aja with concierge. I have Rivven and Raven Royce here asking to speak with you?" she informed him.

His voice started to come in starts and stutters; nothing that we could definitively make out. Finally, the concierge turned to us and said "I'm sorry girls; he's indisposed at the moment. Can I leave a message with him and he can come find you when he's able?"

"Absolutely!" I smiled widely, before letting it drop from my face as I snatched the phone out of her hand. "Please let Mr Bentley know that as the attorney for Ventura Estate, he is our attorney, and if he does not immediately make himself available to us, he will be fired as our lawyer, and as such, will not be entitled to any expenses, including the hotel room he is currently using!"

There was a two second wait before: "Room 506," and the phone clicked as he hung up. I tentatively placed the phone back on its cradle, a satisfied smile on my face as we walked away from the stunned concierge.

"Technicalities," Rogue mumbled. "I like it."

We took the elevator to the fifth floor and found 506. I knocked loudly. Gerard Bentley answered, wearing dishevelled boxer shorts under a hotel bathrobe.

"This is disgusting!" Rogue cried as we pushed our way past him and into the room.

"What do you care? You don't have to clean it!" Gerard snapped.

"We're not interested in your living state," I said flatly, pulling out my phone and dialling. "This is the number for the local police. You give us the key to Ventura Estate, then you disappear, and we won't have you arrested for abusing your authority and shirking your responsibility."

He began to sputter in outrage. "WHAT IS THIS?" he eventually roared.

"You told our Uncle where we were going and where we were staying! You took a bribe from our Uncle to give him the key as soon as you get your hands on it tomorrow morning.

Both are acts that can imprison you for a long, long time! The key, or jail? Your choice!" Rogue yelled.

The lawyer bristled at her speech. "It is also a legal requirement to escort you there and open the estate myself!"

"Well, I can assure you, we won't have you charged for that one. You are going home. You're not to know where Ventura Estate is, nor are you to ever set foot inside the estate should you ever find out, or you'll be charged with trespassing! Now, first thing in the morning we will all be at the office to collect the key, then you will leave," I ordered.

"In return," Rogue stepped in. "We won't have you charged or disbarred."

Gerard didn't move. "DIALLING," I announced.

"OK FINE," he screamed, sitting himself down on his bed with his head in his hands. He groaned, then looked up, a defeated look in his eyes. "Be ready at eight thirty. The taxis will be here then."

"Pleasure doing business with you," I nodded, heading for the door. Once in the hallway, I redialled the police station.

§

"HE WAS ARRESTED?" my mother screeched when we told her upon her and Dad's return to the room. Both of them were gobsmacked at the rapid change of circumstance.

"He was shoddy, Mum. It had to be done or Uncle Reiner would've gotten the key to Ventura Estate, found the deed, and signed it before we could," Rogue explained. Mum shook her head and sat down. Dad appeared pensive but stayed silent.

"We need to leave first thing in the morning, to get to the lawyer's office first. We can't risk getting there after them," I planned, thinking out loud. "The taxis were meant to be here at eight thirty. We cancel the order, rebook one for eight, then, make sure Uncle Reiner and Aunty Regina aren't in it."

CHAPTER 4
Stern, Pierce & Hyde

§§

Six o'clock rolled around and Rogue and me, completely wired, were wide awake and ready to execute the plan. We were fully packed and had called a bellhop to take our bags downstairs to await the taxi. While Mum and Dad were still sleeping, we snuck out of the room and took the elevator to the top floor. The Penthouse; the only suite that was ever good enough for their majesties Reiner and Regina Royce.

"Do you have it?" Rogue whispered as we crept through the foyer.

In response, I pulled out a red card that read: HOUSE-KEEPING MASTER.

"I can't believe you can just do that without thinking," she mumbled back. I shrugged. I did what I had to when I had to. I placed the card into the door slot and the red light turned green. Rogue gently pushed on the door and it glided open soundlessly.

"Penthouse," I grinned, wagging my eyebrows. We were about to make sure there was no way Reina and her family were going to be able to find us.

§

"The taxi has arrived, Miss Royce and Miss Royce. Are you ready?" the bellhop asked.

"Is our luggage loaded?"

"Yes ma'am."

"Mum! Dad! Ready?" Rogue called out. Mum waved from the café, picking up her and Dad's drinks, while Dad followed behind on his phone.

"I understand. We're also glad everything was sorted and resolved before it became a larger issue for all of us," Dad was saying. He'd been on the phone most of the morning trying to get an out of hours contact for the lawyer's office. As it happened, after the police had contacted the managing partner about Mr Bentley, he'd immediately got in contact with Dad himself.

We all filed out of the main hotel doors and as we were piling into the taxi, a concierge came running out to our bellhop. "David! We need you at the Penthouse!"

"Oh?" David responded, looking from the concierge to us. "Ok?"

"We'll be fine from here, dear," Mum said, a concerned look on her face. "You go on." He smiled graciously and closed the car door. "Girls… why would there be such an urgent situation in the Penthouse?"

"Maybe they're trying to leave early too," Rogue suggested. "Go!" The taxi driver pulled out of the hotel drop off and pick up point and headed down the drive.

"Or maybe Reina has demanded a full four course breakfast served immediately." I continued.

"Or Uncle Reiner needs a suit urgently pressed?~"

"~Or maybe… just maybe… we cut the phone cord, put superglue over the security buzzer, tossed their phones down the laundry chute, and broke the door lock so they couldn't get the doors open," I admitted quickly. Mum's mouth dropped open.

"Girls!" Dad admonished. "Do you have any idea what you've done?" he paused for a moment. "…That's a lot of financial damage to the hotel."

I laughed at his lack of interest in the trauma to his brother's family. "I know, but we left a letter with reception to be read only when we'd left admitting our prank and ensuring all costs would be paid for if they sent an invoice to the law firm. We'll ask them to write a cheque when we get the key."

"That's something at least," Dad sighed, rubbing his eyes.

"And how exactly do you think your Grandmother would feel about you using your inheritance for a prank?" Mum asked.

"To be honest, I think Grandma would've thought it was hilarious," I answered.

"And it was necessary to guarantee her wishes are fulfilled," Rogue insisted. "By delaying their ability to leave, we ensure the names on the deed are ours and Grandma gets what she wanted. It wasn't pretty, but it needed to be done."

"And we are taking responsibility for it by making sure they can repair all the damages," I pointed out. Mum went quiet and stared out of the window. I knew she wasn't happy about what we'd done. She was an honourable woman; someone who thought that integrity was the highest of virtues; too honest for her own good. I'm sure she still believed Uncle Reiner would do the right thing and back down if given the opportunity and that, as family, we owed it to him to give him that opportunity. Maybe she was right, but Rogue and I weren't willing to risk Ventura on it.

The rest of our trip passed in silence, with us pretty much all thinking the same thing. Was it the right thing to do? How bad would the damage actually be? Could we be arrested for criminal damage even if we had said we'd pay for it all? And, most importantly… was it going to work?

Too often I found myself feeling dizzy, only to realise I was holding my breath. I hadn't been this anxious since my first summer camp when I was ten. I've never coped well with new social situations and I depended on Rogue to get me through them. My first summer camp was for kids with social problems, so that meant no Rogue. It was my first and only experience being apart from her. I'd lasted one night. One sleepless night, before begging my parents to come and get me, promising that I would absolutely work on developing my social skills, but I needed to do it from a safe and familiar place.

That probably explained why I was so anxious. This was the most unfamiliar, unsafe situation I'd ever been in. I don't know how I would have coped had Rogue not been by my side. I didn't have the chance to figure out how to get my breathing under control before the taxi pulled to a halt and the driver announced we'd arrived.

"Mr Royce, I cannot apologise enough for what happened with Mr Bentley," a man in a suit began hurriedly as he opened the taxi door to let Dad out. "Please, come inside." He then opened the door for Mum and led us through the wide, glass doors.

Mason Pierce was one of three managing partners at Stern, Pierce and Hyde. He was on the shorter side with sandy blonde hair. He was neatly groomed and had a freckly complexion currently wearing an agitated scowl as he led us into an office and directed us to take a seat. "You can rest assured you have the full support of the firm and that your legal matters will be protected with the highest levels of discretion. I personally plan to see out your case myself, and only managing partners will be privy to your information." He took a seat behind the large carved mahogany desk.

"We appreciate your fast action on the matter, Mr Pierce," Mum responded with a kind smile, placing her hand over the top of Dad's comfortingly. "We're just glad everything worked out as it should."

"Yes," Dad agreed. "At the end of the day, I just want my mother's will upheld and my girls to receive their inheritance as it directs."

"And we will do whatever is legally necessary to do just that," Mr Pierce nodded matter of factly, clearly pleased that we weren't threatening to sue. "After what are illegal actions on the part of your brother, I can assure you that he wouldn't have a leg to stand on in court if he were to challenge Reina's will, and if he were to try it, I would be the one arguing in front of the judge myself." His face dropped slightly. "Your mother was a remarkable woman. I'm honoured to have known her."

"Thank you," Dad replied. "She certainly wasn't the type to consider anyone 'the help'. If you were a part of her life, you were family, and she treated you as such."

"Too right she did," Mr Pierce agreed. He then turned to his filing cabinet and drew out a thick file and a wooden lockbox, before turning to Rogue and me. "Shall we?" I took a deep breath as Rogue nodded.

"Ok, so this file is Ventura's entire legal history; from the initial plans and council submissions to the transfer paperwork from each owner to the new one. This lockbox" he shook the wooden box, "-contains the only key to the estate."

"Ok, so what happens now?" Rogue asked breathlessly.

"The lockbox has a combination lock that changes with each new owner. Your grandmother made this combination your birthday, so if you just put that in there…" he explained. I took the box and put in the six digit code. The lock clicked open. "Ah! There we are!"

I slowly lifted the lid to reveal a large, aged, brass key. Despite the high level of care with which the key was always handled, you could tell it was starting to tarnish. "So… that's it? We just take it?"

"That's it!" Mr Pierce nodded with a smile. "I can escort you to the estate immediately. I have the chopper booked and ready. Once there, I'll need to sight the deed with your signatures, and I'll be able to give you the transfer paperwork to sign. Then, it's just a matter of lodging them with the courts and ownership will be officially transferred."

I let out a sigh of relief, but Rogue appeared troubled. "You don't know where she kept the deed, do you?" she asked edgily.

Mum and Dad looked expectantly at Mr Pierce. "No," he replied uncertainly. "I'm sorry, I don't. I'm sure she would have left it in a secure place that you'll be able to locate readily enough to ensure a timely transfer."

I nodded. Let the hunt begin, I thought. "Ok," I said out loud. "Let's go."

"Let's go," Mr Pierce repeated, positively chipper. He led us out of the office and into the elevator.

We were taken via a sleek, black town car to an airfield, where a four blade chopper was waiting for us, just starting its engine. We clambered aboard none too gracefully and buckled ourselves in. Rogue was breathing heavily. She did not do well with heights.

"You'll be ok," I promised, squeezing her hand. "If you go down, I'll go with you," I joked.

"Don't!" she growled back, but she didn't let go of my hand. That was how it was with Rogue and me. We were each strong where the other was weak, pulling each other up when it was needed, supporting each other when the other faltered. We were two halves of a functional human being. It was part of the reason we worked so well together and struggled so much apart.

In less than an hour, we were flying over the forests that covered the southern corner of Ventura Estate. The colours ranged from lime to a deep bottle green. It was incredible.

To the east, we could see the ocean. The waves were crashing against the shore with the incoming afternoon tide. Though we couldn't see it yet, the ocean curved around to the east and went north, creating the cliffs of the coastline.

Atop these cliffs were the Ventura Towers; at the very edge of Ventura Estate; three lighthouses in varying heights. These were designed and built to protect the Ventura coastline against ships.

The further north you went, the smaller the cliffs became until it met the soft grasses of the Ventura Fields. Here, at the northern tip of the estate, the ground dropped into a shallow cove that was always calm and quiet compared to the eastern bay.

To the west, there was a densely overgrown area, which we knew used to be Rief Village, where Raven and Raphael died in the fire that razed the entire area when the Estate was only recently finished. It was now referred to as the 'Burned Village'. Over time, the burned area became soft again and the new grass shoots began to grow. The only place that hadn't been reclaimed by nature was the village centre, which was paved in stone and had a large empty fountain in the middle, its statues and figurines worn and cracked with age.

Just past the village, also currently out of sight, were the Ventura Hills; vast rises of grassy mountains that we knew to be covered in wildflowers at this time of the year. These hills sloped down into the fields from the west.

Despite the glory of the lands that were Ventura Estate, none of these wonders could compare to what lay in its centre. As we flew over the last of the trees, it came into view.

It was almost glowing in the sun's rays. No matter how often we came here, the sight always awed us… and now it was ours. The heart of what had been left to us: the castle of Ventura.

CHAPTER 5

Ventura Estate

§§

The chopper had gone. We were alone with our luggage by the front doors of the majestic Ventura Castle. Seven floors high, it was a warren of countless bedrooms, bathrooms, studies, kitchens, and sunrooms; a sauna, a conservatory, a library, an exterior outlook, and a partridge in a pear tree. Quite literally; Grandma had bred the birds and they lived in the orchard by the fields. It was all ours, and now we could find out why. After, of course, we settled the more urgent matter of finding the deed and signing our names.

The doors were two huge slabs of walnut that towered five feet above us, both intricately carved with the most detailed designs I had ever seen. I stepped forward and took the key from my front pocket. It seemed to tingle at my touch as it slid smoothly into the lock. I took a deep breath before turning it. It gave a loud and echoing click, and the doors swung inward as silently as the Penthouse at the Ricadonna. I finally released the breath, before picking up my suitcase and stepping onto the ledge of the doorstep.

The first thing I saw was the familiar grand marble staircase that led to the upper floors. It was widest at the bottom and narrowed the further up you went, before splitting into two that led in either direction. It was also the last thing I saw as I crossed the threshold and immediately fell to the floor, my vision going black.

When I could see again, I wasn't in the front foyer anymore. I was in a village… and it was burning. One woman ran past me. She was in a lot sharper focus than the others and appeared to be surrounded by a golden glow. She looked a lot like my Aunty Rhiannon had: short, with a round face and brown freckles covering every inch of skin that was exposed, but her hair was jet black instead of straw blonde. Her dark brown eyes were wide and fearful. I knew just from looking that this was her. I'd seen her picture enough throughout my life. This was my namesake. This was Raven… and she was in danger.

There was a yell behind me and I spun around to find Raphael, who looked like a younger version of Dad. He was clean shaven and there was no grey in his hair. He was running towards Raven, who screamed at the sight of him and fled to a nearby house. The sound was muffled like I had earplugs in. I shook my head, trying to hear better, but nothing changed.

As she reached the threshold of the house, more fire erupted from it as the roof caved in. A billowing gust of thick, black smoke tumbled through the door. Raven was thrown backward onto the ground. She raised her head and locked eyes with Raphael, clasping her hand to a wound in her side. In moments, the fire and smoke had engulfed her.

With one last, heart-piercing cry, I was wrenched away. It was like my skin and muscle were being pulled from my bones. When my vision came back into focus I was back in the castle. It was a room I hadn't been before. The walls appeared to be solid gold. I was standing a few feet away from Raphael. He was muttering under his breath, but I couldn't hear what he was saying. I saw him raise his hands, then I was blinded by an explosion of golden light and he appeared to disintegrate.

I was ripped away once more and when I opened my eyes, I was lying on the marble floor of the castle foyer. "RANGER!" I could hear Rogue bellowing at me, while she violently shook my arm. I groaned and looked towards her, everything slowly coming into focus. Mum and Dad were standing over me.

"I'm ok," I grumbled. "Just a little woozy. I'm fine."

"You go and lay down, right now," Mum ordered, her eyes stern.

"But the deed!" Rogue and I cried out together.

"NOW!"

I let go of my suitcase and followed Rogue. We passed the study door and walked into the main foyer. After taking a right at the staircase we headed down the long, wide corridor of the first floor.

Had we turned left, we would have passed the kitchen and the main entrance to one of the living areas. At the very end of that hallway was the doorway that led down into the depths of the castle.

Just past the giant library doors on our right was a spiral staircase. At the top was the room that had always been ours. It wasn't actually a room, but a loft area for the library, with a banister overlooking the library where the fourth wall should have been.

This was the place that felt right to us. What we'd always been told, from our earliest years, was that knowledge was power. That was why it was the library that drew our attention, and why we used this area for our room.

Two walls were straight; one of which held the door that led out onto the second floor landing. The third wall was curved, made entirely of stone, and the only thing on the other side was the Venturan Fields and open air, which could be seen through the window of a large wooden door that led out onto a balcony.

Other than our room, the second floor had other bedrooms, and the outlook. The outlook was a very special part of the castle. The door at the end of the corridor that led to it was made of solid steel for two reasons. The first was that it was a weakness in the castle's fortifications and therefore, was the place most likely to be broken into.

The second, and the reason behind this weakness, was the room on the other side of the large metal door. Like our room, it only had three walls. Where the fourth would have been, where the castle's outer walls *should* have been, were six stone, load bearing pillars that held up the next five floors. A waist high stone barrier filled the spaces in between the pillars, acting as a safety rail.

The outlook room was completely open to the elements, which was why the metal door was needed. It was truly a remarkable piece of architecture. Its north-eastern view included the Venturan Fields and the three lighthouses that were the Towers of Ventura.

"What happened?" Rogue said in a low voice. The way she delivered the question made it clear she wouldn't accept anything but the full answer.

I slowly turned to her. "Raphael..." I started. "The ancestor that first lived here? He didn't die with Raven in the village fire."

"What?" she gasped in disbelief. "How could you possibly know that?"

I took a deep breath and slowly sat on my bed. "When I walked through the doors I got this... this weird feeling. It was like my soul was freezing over, then everything went black," I continued. "I was in the village the night it burned down. Raven was running from Raphael. She was terrified of him. *She* died in the fire, but Raphael didn't. Then I was here, in the castle, and Raphael was standing in a golden room. He was talking to himself, then he started to glow. Then he just… disappeared in a burst of light.”

Rogue stared at me as though I were crazy. “…There's no golden room in the castle, Ranger,” she said slowly.

“Not that we've seen,” I corrected her. “But do you really think all of this is a coincidence? My vision? A mysterious room we've never been in before despite our years exploring here as kids?” I became more frantic the more desperate I felt. Rogue started to shake her head.

“None of Grandma's three kids were left the estate. Instead, it was left to us? Something is happening here; something big, and we're involved somehow and Grandma knew it! We just have to figure out how we fit in. It's all connected!”

Rogue simply stared back at me mournfully, as though she were now also grieving my sanity.

§

“Why would Raphael want to kill Raven?” Rogue asked me for the thousandth time in a week, sliding off the study desk and into her chair. “They were married with a baby. He loved her.”

“I don't know,” I told her again with a groan. “But I don't think Grandma Reina knew. She knew we were meant to have

Ventura, but she didn't understand why any more than we did."

We were lounging around the seventh floor study, the room that always lured Rogue from bed in the middle of the night. She would pass the kitchen on the sixth floor for a snack then spend hours up here reading. Its large bay window was perfect for watching storms and it was where Rogue would spend hours sketching the local wildlife and whatever else took her imagination's fancy. All of her drawings were hung on the wall beside the window.

Currently, the wall was littered with all her pinned up drawings of Raven and Raphael that had kept her nights busy for the past week, in between all the hours we'd spent combing the castle for the deed, which, to our growing dread, still hadn't been found. We'd searched every floor, every bedroom, every study; even the second kitchen with grand dining room and the main foyer that overlooked the sixth floor.

We'd been sitting around for a while, going through book after book on Ventura's history. There were biographies about several of our ancestors who had lived remarkable lives, Romira's diaries that spanned almost fifty years, the local area histories, and books written by Ventura's different owners over the years. It seemed like a trend that ran in the family, as there were three different authors in the last hundred years alone, all having written children's fantasy stories about all manner of creatures from dragons to vampires, and even mermaids and fairies.

There was one book that particularly interested me. It was a book of maps and blueprints. The centre pages were a map of the castle and its grounds.

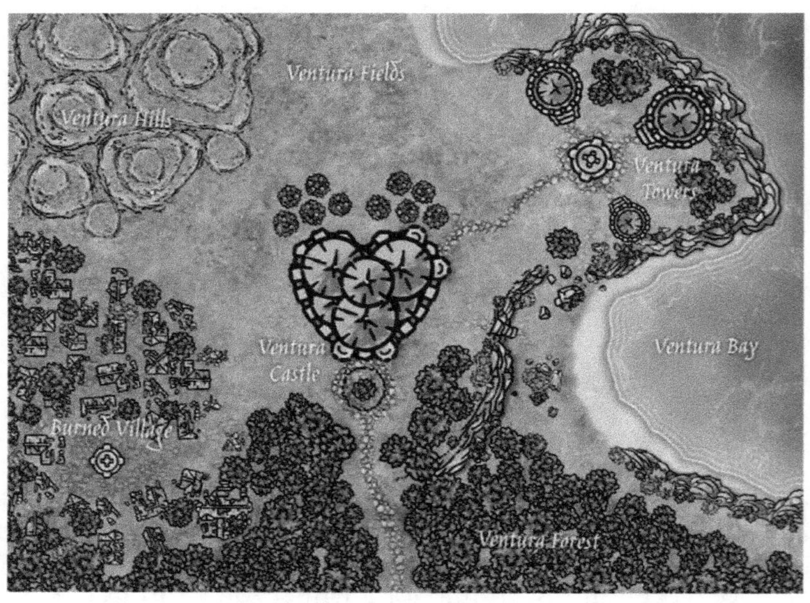

"Rogue... Have a look at this," I breathed.

She stepped over and looked at the page. "Whoa... What's with that?" she asked in a hushed whisper.

"It's... a heart. All of the curved walls and we never questioned what the castle was shaped like. It's a heart," I said. "I just thought it was a circle."

"The Heart of Ventura… I've heard that reference before; I'm sure of it," Rogue frowned, deep in thought. Suddenly, she leapt to her feet and began pulling books off the shelves, discarding one after the other as she checked the titles. "No. No… No… No. N- YES!" She squeezed it to her chest before turning around and showing it to me. It was an ancient volume covered with black leather… and a deep slash right across the cover that went almost all the way through, revealing the red binding underneath. She opened it and began to read.

When Romira Royce first founded Ventura Estate, he set out to build an empire; an empire that would be free from all rule. First came the forests. The trees were few, so he ordered four thousand saplings to be planted in the south, and as they grew, they became the Forests of Ventura.

Then, there was the village. For those he loved and those who loved him; for those who were in his employ, he built houses. When it was finished, he gave the village people what was to be called the 'Eternal Flame', a torch that would, one day, rival the Olympic Flame. It burned, day and night, in the empty fountain foundation in the village centre.

Next, were the mountains to the north-west. From the moment Romira set foot upon the land, the hills began to flower until the day came when you could no longer see any green through all the colours that covered the Hills of Ventura.

At the north eastern most point of Ventura Estate, he built three differently sized lighthouses. It is believed that the Towers of Ventura represented himself, and his twin children, whom, Romira claimed, were destined to protect Ventura after him.

The north and the eastern regions of Ventura Estate, Romira let be. They were the fields and the sea, always to be there as nature intended them. At the edge of the fields, Romira himself planted tree saplings that would grow into Ventura's orchard.

It was only when the work was completed, however, that he began its focal point. Nestled in the very centre of Ventura Estate, between the ocean, the forest, the hills and the orchard, was to be the architectural masterpiece that is now Ventura Castle. The Heart of Ventura, where the Royce family could govern the land, but never rule it, for all were free in Ventura Estate.

It was when the fourth floor was being constructed that tragedy befell Romira, and he lost his life. It is said that with his death came a blinding flash of light and his heart came apart from his body. The heart became one with the castle; the true Heart of Ventura.

Rogue finished and whistled, "Whoa."

"I saw that golden light in my vision when Raphael disappeared… but that still doesn't explain what I saw. Why would Raphael want Raven, his wife, dead?" I asked.

"Maybe she tried to steal the Heart?" Rogue considered.

"No," I said immediately. "It was definitely Raphael who was up to something. Raven was terrified… and all the villagers? They weren't running from Raven."

"They were running from a fire, and bad guys can get pretty terrified when they're cornered, too," Rogue pointed out. "We don't know enough about what you saw to make any judgements yet."

This was the first time Rogue had acknowledged my 'vision', or whatever it was, as something more than a crazy dream I had after passing out. "So you believe me?" I asked.

"I don't not believe you," she answered slowly. "I agree, it's odd that Ventura was left to us given the number of adults around ready, willing, and able to claim it. I agree that you dropping the second you walk in the door is weird. I agree that there is definitely something up with our family history that is suspicious… I believe you saw what you saw. I don't know if I'm ready to agree it was necessarily real," she murmured finally. "And it is definitely weird that this book describes Romira dying in a blast of light when that's exactly how you saw Raphael go in your vision, or dream, or whatever."

I tilted my head slightly in a slow nod. "I'll take what I can get, I guess."

Rogue stayed quiet. "What if Raphael didn't like governing the people and wanted to rule?" she suggested after a time. "What if he needed the Heart to do it? Oh!" she gasped. "What if he killed Romira?"

"His own father?" I questioned with a frown. "I suppose… If you're evil enough to use your father's heart to rule people, you're evil enough to kill him for it."

"Do you really believe the Heart story? The golden light and all that?" Rogue asked.

"If you'd seen it too, you wouldn't need to ask. I saw the light completely take over Raphael somewhere here in the castle before he exploded. It could have been the magic of Romira's heart destroying the evil in the castle. That's what the Heart would be for, to protect Ventura Estate. Romira loved all the people in his care. The Heart wouldn't have stood for what Raphael was doing if he were trying to take over, especially if it were his father's," I explained, pulling apart what we knew, piece by piece.

"So we believe in magic now?" Rogue grumbled in response, before sighing. "We need to know more."

"We don't know where to look for any more information," I told her exasperatedly. "We've been through every book in the library and every study in the castle. Hell, we even went through the *cookbooks* in both of the kitchens! What else is there?"

"We were given information through a vision before. It could always happen again. If the Heart killed Raphael, maybe it's the Heart that's trying to give us information. It wants us to have it. Once it realises we don't have enough, it'll give us more," Rogue stated logically.

"So you agree it was a vision?" I questioned again.

"This Heart business can't be a coincidence," she replied, rubbing her eyes tiredly. "And this version of the burning village story explains a lot more than the other one; like the fact that if everybody died, how would anybody have known Raphael and Raven were even there? For all anybody knew, they'd just run away together and disappeared."

I started to think and after a second, I thought of something. "What if it wasn't the Heart sending me the vision?" I asked. "What if… and bear with me here… it was Raven?"

"What do you mean?" Rogue frowned.

"Well, if a centuries old golden heart can survive to send visions, isn't it a lot more logical that spirits can do it better?" I explained.

"The cold chill…" Rogue whispered, her voice drifting off as she gazed at nothing.

"Her reaching out?" I suggested. "Or Raphael trying to stop her from getting to us?"

"Well, if she tried once, she'll try again. Obviously, somebody or something somewhere wants us to know the truth. We'll work it out eventually. We just have to wait until she contacts us again," Rogue concluded.

What we didn't plan on was the Heart of Ventura becoming the last thing on our minds, as we heard the echo of a scream from many floors below.

CHAPTER 6

Secrets

§§

It was a high pitched scream. Inaudible words were issuing from her mouth. She was soaked to the bone, and Dad didn't seem to care. "What on earth is the matter with you?" he asked Reina, his finger massaging his left ear.

Reina took a deep breath and stared murderously up at us, perched on the railing overlooking the main atrium from the second floor. Dad had insisted we not come down when he heard them coming.

"YOU TOOK THE CHOPPER WE WERE *ALL* SUPPOSED TO GO IN, SO WE HAD TO PAY FOR A WEEK'S STAY AT THE HOTEL BEFORE WE COULD GET THE NEXT ONE! NOW THAT WE'RE HERE, YOU DON'T ANSWER THE DOOR AND LEAVE US IN THE RAIN FOR AGES!" she screeched.

"Oh, Reina, do stop," Aunty Regina sighed. "We're here and inside now. That's all that matters." Aunty Regina, ever the optimist.

"Maybe you should've screamed louder? We couldn't hear you over the rain," Rogue called down, smiling mischievously. "And the last time I checked, you weren't supposed to be here until next week. We were to come here first and get the castle in order. After *that*, it was open to family. You wouldn't be here right now if you hadn't paid off the lawyer to find out we'd already left."

"*Girls!*" Mum warned, bustling over to them with a handful of towels.

"Have some respect, Rivven!" Uncle Reiner yelled back at the same time.

"Yes, Rogue, do," Dad sighed in an Aunty Regina like fashion. "We all need to be respectful at this difficult time." Uncle Reiner's face was as stormy as the sky outside, but Aunty Regina smiled and nodded appreciatively, missing the joke entirely.

"He can't talk about respect. He doesn't even respect his mother enough to accept her decision," I shot back. With that, I stalked away, leaving them dripping on the stone floor.

§

Summer was bringing with it a heatwave. It had only just ended with this day of nothing but storm clouds and rain. Ten days since we'd arrived here and we'd had no luck finding the deed either. With the rain having died down from the gale it started as and there being very little wind, we had taken to hiding in the outlook. We got to appreciate the view of the fields and the Towers, and the cove further into the distance.

We were outside, experiencing what little breeze the weather had to offer, which was a welcome respite from the stagnant, humid air inside the castle walls. At the top of the list of benefits was that our cousins hated the outlook and avoided it at all costs. "Peaceful, isn't it?" I asked Rogue, rolling my head in her direction.

She glanced up from her latest historical find, a book on hieroglyphs. One of the interior outlook walls was covered in large symbols and characters that weren't in any known language we could find. Rogue had gone ancient, looking for every language book Ventura had, and poring through them one by one in an attempt to decode what was written on the wall.

"No," she said flatly. "We need to find the deed before they catch on that we haven't actually signed it," she snapped, turning the pages aggressively.

"Says the girl procrastinating with a language puzzle that has nothing to do with the deed," I retorted with a laugh.

"You don't know they're not connected!" she exclaimed, not taking her eyes off the page. "For all we know that's a message that will give a clue or even the answer to where we find it!"

I raised an eyebrow. "That is some serious straw grasping Farmer John, but given what I've asked you to believe in recent history, you won't get any arguments from me." I turned back to my own book, which was actually more of a diary. It was the building manager's log from when he was facilitating the build. Rogue had asked me to look up the section describing the building of the outlook, but there was no mention of any writing or carvings of any language being designed for the area.

Once I'd checked that section for her, I had gone back to the beginning and started reading through it, trying to find any mention of any hidden areas, hidey holes, wall safes behind portraits, or anything else out of the ordinary that could be where the deed was kept. There had been some interesting things so far, such as:

Entry 24 LOWER KITCHEN

Master Royce has approved his head cook's request of a second cool room that is only accessible to her for storage of the more valuable products. It is to be placed behind a false wall in the lower kitchen, next to the stove, to be opened via a circular stone at floor level.

No such luck. We went to the kitchen. We found the stone. We pushed it in and heard the tell-tale click of a latch unbarring. After decades of no use, it took both Rogue and I pushing with the entire weight of both our bodies to get the door to shift, and even then, we couldn't get it to open all the way. But it was enough to let us in, and while finding a hidden room full of shelves was definitely interesting, it didn't have what we were looking for, with the exception of a very cold place to relax when the humidity became too much.

Entry 37 FURNACE

Master Royce has requested an additional tunnel leading from the furnace room to the lower regions of the hills, close to the shoreline, as a means to release pressure build up caused by the heat, should the other ducts become blocked.

That was a no go as well. The tunnel entrance was hidden by the furnace, behind a large silver barred gate. Though we were able to get the gate open, the tunnel itself was non-existent. Either the builders were never able to start the construction, Romira changed his mind about wanting a tunnel, or it had caved in. Whatever the reason, it was a dead end of dirt and stone.

Entry 56 LOWER SUNROOM

Master Royce has approved Lady Romana's request of a means of escape from the castle in times of danger. Passage to be through the stone floor, along the rock bed, and into the TOWERS site foundations being built in the north-eastern region of the estate. Entry via the left sconce on the south western wall.

That one was cool. At first, we couldn't figure it out. "Which one is the south western wall?"

"Are we sure we have the right sunroom?"

"It says lower!"

"Left from which direction? From our point of view or the sconces'?"

"What do we do? Push? Pull? Twist?"

It was a left turn, so the whole sconce tilted sideways, making it look as though it were falling off the wall. As soon as it clicked into place, a grinding sound began and our feet started to vibrate. Over in the corner, one of the carpet runners started to move, lowering from its place on the floor until it disappeared completely.

We were amazed. The floor had lowered in sections underneath the carpet, creating a stone stairway that led down into a perfectly preserved, save for a few cobwebs, escape tunnel. It was fully lined in stone, wide enough for three people to walk side by side, and had torch sconces evenly placed along the left hand side of the tunnel as far as we could see, which was not very far given none of them were lit. We had spent almost an entire night running along the tunnel, clearing out the cobwebs, checking the walls for clues to any other tunnels, or writing, like we'd found in the outlook.

At the end, there was a raised stone on the floor. Rogue stepped on it and stone panels from above us started to lower, creating a replica stone staircase to the one that had led us down into the tunnel. At the top, we found ourselves looking out a bay window and across the stormy ocean. The tunnel had led us into the largest of the three lighthouses known as Ventura Towers. An awesome find, and very exciting, but given the deed was only ever kept in the castle, we knew we wouldn't find what we were looking for there.

So, I'd continued reading. We'd investigate every new find with the expected vigour, but we were still becoming somewhat disheartened at our lack of success. If Grandma Reina had left any clue to where the deed was, we couldn't see it, and if it was meant to be obvious, then we couldn't figure out what we were missing. I didn't know which I found more frustrating, until:

Entry 78 LIBRARY

Master Royce has requested the nook in the library be made to double thickness to

allow for storage behind the shelving for all vitally important documents and

keepsakes.

"ROGUE!" I screeched, getting up and bolting to the library. Rogue was at my heels in an instant, no questions asked.

In the little nook that curved around the left hand side of the library, was a glass cabinet. I gingerly eased the door open and shifted the contents to the side, feeling around for something, anything that could give away the access point to what was inside. Rogue stood at my side, breathing heavily, eyes wide. The carved wooden edging around the shelves had more of the same symbols as what was in the outlook, but I ignored that completely. We were close… I knew it.

"Yes!" I cried out, as a piece of the decorative edging slid to the side and the back of the shelf fell forward, revealing a wooden box and an ancient looking book that had probably been put there by a past Royce who had wanted to preserve it.

We only had eyes for the box. I eased it out of its place on the shelf and held it in my arms. Rogue pushed the clasp on the front of the box and it clicked open. She lifted the lid slowly and took a deep breath in, before removing two pieces of paper. One was a letter in an envelope. The other was a thick scroll; the deed.

"Over here!" I hissed, running to the table in the corner and placing the box down. "Find a pen! Quick!" I took the envelope from Rogue as she began rummaging in the desk for a pen to sign the deed with. I pulled the letter out of the envelope and began to read.

To my Rogue and Ranger,

Hello, my darlings! I know that when you read this, I'll be gone, but, as long as I know it is you who holds my Heart, I can die happy. I know this must be a very confusing time for you both, and for that, I'm sorry. I hope you know that if I could have held on longer, I would have. I only want good things for you girls, and I know that giving you the responsibility of Ventura Estate will effectively end your childhood far too prematurely.

The Castle of Ventura and the surrounding Estate is what means the most to me, and if it is to mean the most to you, you must understand why it was left to you two. When I was a child, my parents would often take trips away. When they returned from one such trip, they brought with them an orphaned boy. While the boy was perfectly healthy, he had no memory of where he had come from or who he was, and my parents never discussed it.

Not long after his arrival, I had a vision. Now, I understand that I may sound out of my mind, but there it is. Our ancestor, Raven, came to me, claiming twin girls, a Rogue and a Ranger, would soon be born to the family; the first twins since Romira's to be born. She said that it was to be you two that could undo the horrific crime she had committed and end what she had started. She could not explain to me what she meant, but told me 'Everything is behind one good deed'. I didn't know what she meant, but I know you can find out.

I grew up and almost forgot about the vision until I married your grandfather, that same boy my parents had brought home not a decade before! I became pregnant with your Uncle Reiner and remembered the vision, wondering if these were the twin girls I was told to expect. But no, you two came a generation later.

I don't know what crime she believes she committed. I don't know what you are meant to do from here, if anything at all, other than take care of the estate, as I did in my time, but she foresaw you and made it clear that Ventura's future was in your hands. This is why it is yours now, and while I don't know what is next for you, I do know that exactly who and what you are will keep Ventura on the right path.

Good luck, my children. I love you. Grandma Reina.

"Wow," Rogue breathed softly. "So Raven took a liking to hauntings long before you, huh?" She stood there, the scroll under her arm; a finally found pen in her hand.

"The deed!" I gasped, lunging forward.

"Oh yeah!" She fumbled with the scroll as she struggled to unroll it without dropping the pen, like if she did, she might never find another one. She placed a pencil holder and a book on the top two corners, before slowly rolling out the remainder of the scroll. It was a thick, soft animal skin. The words seemed to be just as vibrant as the day they had been printed:

TITLE DEED: VENTURA ESTATE & GROUNDS

THIS DEED IS TO HEREBY CLAIM AND CERTIFY OWNERSHIP OF THE VENTURA ESTATE, TO BE SIGNED BY EACH OWNER AS IT IS PASSED DOWN THROUGH THE ROYCE FAMILY.

My breath caught in my throat. There it was; the answer, the goal, and the deed. "I can't believe it's here," Rogue whispered.

Slowly, respectfully, she and I signed our names alongside the others. We returned the deed to the box and eased it back onto the shelf with an emotionally exhausted groan.

"One question forward, five questions back," I huffed. Rogue picked up the letter and together, we walked back to our room, where we sat and read it, over and over again: Everything is behind one good deed. "She said that she'd committed a crime, so that can't be the good deed. Rather contradictory," I sighed.

"We'll figure it out," Rogue yawned.

CHAPTER 7
Raven's Letter

§§

That night, I dreamed.

Raphael is sitting at a desk, signing a document, a smile on his face. It's the deed. There's a flash and I'm somewhere different. Raven is bathed in a golden glow. She's holding something in her hand. It's slowly pulsing in her grip. She closes her eyes and takes a deep breath in, before holding it to her chest and running from the room.

I awoke in a veil of sweat, short of breath. "What is it?" Rogue asked roughly, pulling herself out of bed. "What happened?"

"Raven took the Heart," I gasped, wiping my forehead. "I saw her take it."

"Another vision?"

"It was a dream, but I think so."

"So she did take it," Rogue said. "Raphael was trying to get it back!"

"Yes." I shook my head. "She took it, but it was to get it away from him. He wanted it for something she couldn't let him use it for."

"What makes you think that?" she questioned, folding her arms.

"I saw him signing the deed; the look on his face. Ventura wasn't meant to be his; I could tell. It was… smug, arrogant; like he was getting away with something," I told her.

"Where do you think the Heart was kept? Where was Raven when she took it?" Rogue asked me.

"Raven was in the same golden room I saw Raphael in when he died. We haven't found a single place like that… but the book said that it became a part of the castle," I said as I remembered.

"Yes, but for Raven to have gotten her hands on it, then it had to actually be kept somewhere," Rogue put in. "Maybe it didn't stay here."

"There was something else," I went on, biting my lip. "I saw Raphael signing the deed at a desk; the same desk in the library corner where we signed it. Like I said, he was smiling. The deed… The good deed…" I drifted off.

"You think the good deed… is the estate deed?" Rogue asked me.

"I don't see why it can't be," I answered, climbing out of bed. She followed me as I headed for the spiral staircase. We ran down it, skipped the last four steps, and tore around the corner, re-opening the glass cabinet and its hidden compartment.

"Behind the good deed," Rogue breathed, as I began to pull everything out. Dawn had just broken and light was streaming in through the library windows from the east. We removed the box and began pressing all of the wood around it. After an hour, Rogue was close to tearing the cabinet off the wall. "It's not here!" she yelled. "Whatever we're looking for, it's not here!"

"Behind the good deed," I quietly repeated. "If the good deed is the estate deed, then~" I began. I was cut off by the sound of Reina yelling from the front foyer. "What does she want now?" I groaned.

Once in the foyer, we found Reina surrounded by shopping bags. As the last bags were unceremoniously dropped on the floor, Aunty Regina walked in, folding her umbrella.

"What?" Rogue said flatly.

"Have these dealt with, will you?" Reina demanded coolly, pulling off her coat and dumping it with the bags. She and her mother then gave us a huge smile; Reina's, snotty and pretentious; Aunty Regina's, more genuine, but still entitled; before they both disappeared into the kitchen, leaving us alone with the bags. Rogue and I turned to each other and smiled as well. We then promptly dealt with the bags, hurling each and every one of them out into the rain.

§

That afternoon; after each of the bags had been brought back inside and cleaned; after Dad had scolded us for ruining a lot of money's worth of clothes, magazines, and makeup, and after he'd explained to his brother's family that Rogue and I were not maids to order around; we were back in the library, putting everything back into the cabinet.

"I don't think it meant behind the box," I told her, continuing our morning conversation.

"Well, considering we never found anything, I don't think it ever meant the deed in the first place," Rogue retorted grumpily.

"It said 'behind the good deed', not 'behind where the good deed is kept'," I explained further. "Whatever we're looking for, it's in the box too," I announced, presenting the box with a flourish. We frantically tore everything out of the box and tipped it upside down, tapping the bottom. There was a loud and jarring thud as the bottom fell open and three pieces of paper fell out.

"YES!" Rogue cheered. "We did it! We actually found it!" She danced around on the spot, spinning and clapping.

I picked up one piece, while Rogue grabbed another. The one I had taken was familiar to us. It was the blueprint of the castle and the surrounding grounds. This one, however, was different. "Rogue, look at these," I said. She peered over my shoulder.

"Yeah, it's the grounds. We've seen that," she said dismissively, glancing back to her page.

"But it's not. Look," I prompted. "Parts have been added and others scribbled out.

"What are these? The estate names?" Rogue questioned, getting a better look.

"Draconix…Valeria?" I read. "Why would the castle's name be Sanvicor? It's Ventura Castle."

"And the hills are Ventura Hills and the towers are the Ventura Towers. What if these were their names before they were Ventura Estate?" Rogue put in.

"Maybe," I mumbled. I didn't think so, though. I thought that Romira would've wanted to keep the original names if they'd had any. "What are the other pieces?"

Rogue turned back to the second piece of paper; a letter. She read it out.

Rogue and Ranger,

I am sorry to say that I do not know your real names; just who you are. I know your future; your destiny. I know that it is you, who are to save the lands of Ventura. I know that there is much that you do not know. I write this in haste, unsure of how much time I have. I will endeavour to offer as much knowledge as I can.

My father, Romira, was a magnificent man, who did wondrous things. He was a Sorcerer, of a kind. He was able to wield great magic and was incredibly powerful. Few know this; he did not share it willingly.

You may or may not know that he not only designed and built Ventura Estate but also the Venturan Worlds.

"What?" I interrupted flatly, a dumbstruck look on my face.

"Shh!" Rogue shot back, waving her hand.

Nobody knows why he created these worlds. We believed that he simply wanted to create more wonder and beauty for the world and thought that it would not thrive or exist peacefully here. To the latter, we were correct. The parts of the world that still believes in magic, consider it blasphemous heresy.

The entrance to each of these worlds was a mirror, with each frame made from the material and magic of the world it led to. These were to be kept in the Castle of Ventura. Romira always vowed that he would protect the Venturan Worlds, until time itself ceased to exist, and he weaved his most powerful magicks to do it.

My husband, Raphael, who had always yearned for the power wielded by his father, killed him for it. Romira's heart glowed golden and became the Heart of Ventura, powered by the magic and spirit of Romira. When the castle's final three floors were completed, Raphael's obsession with the worlds reached a pinnacle. There was nothing we could do to turn him away from coveting the worlds Romira had created.

I learned that he was planning to use the Heart of Ventura to take control of Romira's worlds. He had been recruiting soldiers from father's workers, who had finished building the castle and were still living in Rief Village. He planned to take each world, by force, if necessary.

I did what I had to in order to stop him. I stole the Heart. I travelled to each world, offering a warning, and when I got there, I found the Heart would glow, and a part would separate from the whole. Each piece of the Heart was left in the keep of a Guardian.

In Sanvicor, Raphael found me. He has learned that his magic is no match for the Heart of Ventura, no matter how many pieces it is in, but I've been mortally wounded. I am now hiding in Rief Village, knowing my time is ending. The Guardian who holds the Sanvicoran Heart said he would contain Raphael as long as he could, so I could flee.

The moment I was back in Ventura Castle, I hid all seven mirrors. The piece of Romira's heart that is hidden in each world connects to the magic he put into the mirror's frame. This power hides the mirrors from Raphael's magic, as it is designed to protect the worlds from harm, but once he finds me, he'll go looking for the mirrors. I only hope that the Heart's magic is strong enough to protect them.

I have been here two days already, and I know Raphael draws near. I can feel his anger growing as I write this. I cannot say outright, where I have hidden the mirrors, for if it fell into the wrong hands, the consequences could be disastrous. Find the mirrors and reunite the Heart of Ventura. Only then will Raphael be vanquished from its lands.

The worlds are in your hands. The light need not be bright, to shine through the darkest night.

Raven Royce

Silence fell for a long, drawn out minute. "She knew who we were," I finally breathed in awe.

"She knew who we'd be," Rogue corrected me, folding up the letter. "She knew we'd exist one day."

"So… this map isn't the name of Ventura Estate before it was Ventura; it's the map of the other worlds," I said, speaking slowly, trying to take it all in.

"Different worlds… in some kind of dimension parallel to ours, created by our ancestor… who knew magic. That's just a bit more than I can take right now," Rogue groaned, leaning back onto the desk chair, her hands over her face. "Spirits… Visions… Castle…"

"So, what I saw… the golden glow and Raphael disappearing?" I started. "After Raven died, he tried to find the mirrors to get back to the worlds just like Raven said he would, but the magic of the Heart stopped him somehow and he died."

"Well, that's the best we can hope for anyway," Rogue sighed. "Can't imagine what the worlds look like now if he's been ruling them for centuries."

"We have to find out," I said immediately.

"WHAT?" she exclaimed incredulously.

"We have to find the mirrors and go to the worlds!" I squealed excitedly. "And if Raphael hasn't been there, collect the Heart and reunite the pieces!"

"Are you insane?" Rogue cried out.

"Listen," I forced myself to calm down and speak slowly. "Raven saw us coming, somehow. She told Grandma Reina what to name us. When Raven gave me that vision, the cold snap I felt was icy and cold. It was dangerous. However Raphael died, he either didn't stay that way or he did something magically to stick around."

"That doesn't mean we should go looking for him," she hissed.

"The Heart is in pieces and it's meant to be protecting worlds full of other people. If Raphael is still around, he's dangerous to everyone. He'll be after us because just like Raven, he's been waiting for us. We were meant to do this," I explained. "Raven knew it and so did Grandma Reina. It's not going to be easy... but it was always meant to be us."

Rogue closed her eyes and huffed. After a dramatically long pause, she opened her eyes. "Fine."

CHAPTER 8

The Riddle

§§

"How do we even start?" she groaned, unenthused.

I thought for a second. "The riddle!" I looked around the desk, where the box lay, discarded. "Where's the other piece of paper?"

"Here!" she said, picking it up off the floor. She opened it out and held it up so we could read it together.

The fae reside with the setting of the sun,

The first ever of its design;

The wall of coloured glass isn't all it seems,

If it is they you wish to find.

The second can be found where all is cleansed,

This task, you will find, is draining;

Fit for a Queen, it is larger than the rest,

You mustn't keep the merfolk waiting.

The third where nature is lush and full of life,

Where they receive the most light;

The pack will demand its due respect,

For their triumphs and their might.

The fourth is where a century worth of evil,

Has been burned in the dead of night;

Its warmth is both favoured and feared,

Leading to the land of the light.

Though very different from its feathered cousin,

The fifth is also among the heat;

Talon, scale, and flame await you,

Hidden in this humid, leisurely treat.

The sixth is in the open air,

Yet, still within the castle walls;

To lead you to the cloud kingdom,

Flee from here if a storm calls,

The seventh and final is on the seventh and last,

In the castle's Pride of Place,

Return the Heart to the Golden Centre,

To keep Ventura's worlds eternally safe.

"Return the Heart to the Golden Centre…" I read.

"Well, this sounds easy!" Rogue replied sarcastically, right as a window to our right flew open and a hurricane level wind blew through the library; picking up papers, maps, posters, and books alike, and hurling them around the room. At that same moment, the familiar cold chill that I'd felt before froze my breath as I attempted to inhale. "What is that?" Rogue shivered; her voice soft.

"Raphael!" I gasped. "RUN!" Rogue threw herself to the floor and grabbed the one yellowed piece of paper that she could see before we both took off for the main doors. We could still hear the roaring of the wind as we ran. The cold wind billowed around us and made our breath catch in our chests before a forceful, violent gust threw us forward onto the grand staircase as we ran through the atrium.

I hauled Rogue to her feet and we kept on running. We didn't stop until we reached the first floor living room, where we found… everybody. Sitting by the windows, watching the storm, were our parents, aunty, uncle and cousins. All of them were staring at us with shocked expressions as we desperately gulped in air.

"What was that all about?" Dad asked, looking up from his book as he took his glasses off. "What happened?"

"F-fell down the stairs," Rogue gasped, waving her hand. "We're fine."

"Uh, Dad? Mum?" I began, getting an idea. "Can we talk to you?" They got up and followed us out into the hallway. I noticed that the wind had stopped, and the summer humidity had returned.

"What's wrong?" he asked, eyebrows scrunched and eyes concerned.

"We…" I began, not sure how to start. "We don't think the castle is safe." Dad frowned. Mum looked shocked. Rogue looked at me, horrified. "I mean- the pillars in the outlook room have started to crumble. They need to be repaired as soon as possible or- or it could bring down the whole castle," I said quickly. Rogue's face changed from puzzlement to agreement and turned back to Dad, nodding.

"What?" Mum questioned. "Are you sure?"

"The stone is starting to come away. We started noticing it a few days ago when we were out there but didn't think anything of it until we saw that chips were coming away during the storm. We really shouldn't stay here for much longer in case the wind gets stronger," Rogue jumped in.

"We've just moved in!" Dad cried. "We just got here!"

"We'll book rooms at the hotel in town. We've got no choice; it's too dangerous to stay," Mum assured him. As they headed back to the living room to explain to Uncle Reiner what was going on, Rogue and I breathed a sigh of relief.

§

By eight in the morning, the whole family had packed up and headed into town. Rogue and I had insisted on stay behind, convincing Mum and Dad that it had to be us because it was our Estate and therefore, our 'responsibility' to wait for the builder coming to do the inspection.

"We promise we won't go inside," Rogue told Dad. But of course, the second they were out of sight, we ran to the front door. "Man, we're good!" she grinned.

"They'll understand. We had to get them out," I stated breathlessly. "What if Raphael tried to attack them to scare us off?"

"We need to lock every door and window that can be used as an entrance into the Castle," Rogue said. "If we actually find a mirror that sends us to another world, it's obvious Mum and Dad will come looking for us eventually. We need to make sure they can't get in."

"Yeah," I agreed, nodding.

In the front foyer, Rogue pulled the piece of paper she'd managed to catch in the library during the gale out of her pocket. It held the mirror riddle. She reread the first lines. *"The fae reside with the setting of the sun, the first ever of its design; the wall of coloured glass isn't all it seems if it is they you wish to find."*

"A place where we can see the sun and where there's a wall of coloured glass," I said slowly.

"The outlook room."

"There's no coloured glass."

"The conservatory and the sunrooms have stained glass windows," she said. "So does the old chapel."

"The chapel is on the grounds, but not in the castle… but the conservatory and the sunrooms?" I considered thoughtfully. "Which one?"

"We check them all," she said, shrugging her shoulders. The first sunroom was on the first floor, right next to the library. After the events of the previous night, we had been giving it a wide berth, even having slept in the living room instead of our loft.

We crept down the corridor, moving as quickly and quietly as we could as we passed the library, unsure of whether the unexpected, supernatural weather event would repeat itself. Both of us were actively avoiding thinking about how else Raphael may present himself, and where else he just might decide to. We reached the doorway to the sunroom without incident. The entryway was a large open archway that met at the top in a curved point.

Once on the other side, we were met with the large round window that covered most of the back wall. Outside, we could see the sun steadily rising into the sky, peeking out from a multitude of storm clouds. The rest of the room was fairly empty; just a simple floor runner leading to a sitting area by the windows, and a tall leafy plant by the doorway.

"Say the rhyme again," Rogue said.

"*The fae can be found with the setting of the sun.*"

"Check."

"*The first ever of its design.*"

"Ok."

"*The wall of coloured glass isn't all it seems~*"

"~Wait."

"What?"

"The sun," she replied. "It's rising."

"So?" I responded, right as I realised I'd missed a very important word in the riddle.

"This sunroom faces east," she went on, gazing around the room. "It doesn't f~." She was cut off by a loud bang from the atrium, and we felt the beginnings of a breeze brush our faces. She snapped her head back to me and we locked eyes. "Run," she ordered in a deadly soft voice.

We flew from the room as fast as our feet, and the cobbled flagstones of the castle corridors, would allow. As we hit the atrium, Rogue turned and headed for the door.

"*What are you doing?*" I yelled over the growing storm. At this point, we couldn't tell if it was coming from inside or outside.

"RUNNING!" she screamed back. "WHAT ELSE WOULD I BE DOING?"

"We can't leave! This might be our only chance to find the mirror! Who knows what'll happen if we don't find the Heart!" She gave me a silent, terrified look. "THIS IS BIGGER THAN US!" I cried out. She gulped and, after a moment frozen by the front door, nodded.

We ran to the third floor. The moment we hit the top step and came out onto the landing, everything suddenly became very still. It was eerily quiet as we turned left and right, trying to remember which corridor led to the sunroom. As well as the sunroom, Rowan, Reina, Aunty Regina and Uncle Reiner's rooms were on this floor, so we tended to avoid it.

"That way," Rogue whispered, pointing to the left. We lightly ran as fast as we could, trying to make as little noise as possible. At the end of the corridor was the same stone archway that led into the sunroom on the first floor, but this had hieroglyphs carved into the top of the arch; the same kind that we had been attempting to transcribe from the outlook room.

"This is it," I breathed, pointing. We stepped through the arch and into the sunroom. Like the first floor sunroom, the outer wall was entirely made of glass, but instead of large, clear panels overlooking the fields and ocean, multi coloured panels came together to create breathtaking images of landscapes and wildlife. The sunlight pouring into the room left colour dancing across the opposite wall. One image was a leaping horse; another was a woman in a long purple gown with hair that was just as long; another was an underwater scene with brightly coloured fish.

"Ranger," Rogue called. She was standing in front of the very centre image, the one of the woman in the purple dress. I joined her. "Look." She was pointing at the panels where the woman's hair met her dress.

"Wha- Oh!" I gasped, finally seeing the image as it truly was. "That's not hair! It's-"

"~Wings," Rogue finished. "It's a fairy."

"*The fae reside with the setting of the sun*," I quoted, gazing at the glass. I started studying the image feverishly, looking for a clue as to where the mirror could be within it. As the light reflected off the glass, I followed the rays to the opposite wall, where the colours lit up the stone.

There were multiple portraits and tapestries lining the wall, all scattered with light and shadows from the stained glass windows. The purple and pink from the fairy image gave a woman in one of the portraits a rosy glow. As I crept closer, I realised I recognised the woman. It was Raven.

"Rogue!" I hissed. She turned from the stained glass windows and crossed the room in three bounds. "It's Raven!" Shadows from the window image surrounded the portrait. What we always had thought were butterflies, were actually smaller fairies. Pixies? My eyes landed on one particular pixie. It had its arms out, as though it were reaching for the frame of the portrait. Curious, I reached for the frame where the shadow was. There, in the corner, was a single hieroglyph. It looked like an oval with pointed edges and ridges, like a feather or a leaf. "Help me!" I said to Rogue.

We gripped both sides of the frame and lifted it off the wall, shuffling along slightly before lowering it gently to the floor. When we turned back to where the portrait had been, we both gasped. There, reflecting the multicoloured lights, was the first mirror, its surface shining like diamonds.

It was so large; Rogue and I were able to stand beside each other and still see our whole bodies. It covered the entire wall that had been hidden by the portrait. The frame was a dark reddish cedar and engraved with vines and flowers. At the very top, the frame curved upwards to end in a spike. At this tip was a single word. "Valeria," I read.

Suddenly, a low grumbling started under our feet, vibrating our whole bodies. My eyes met Rogue's. "Together?" she asked quickly. I answered by taking her hand and pulling her forward. She gasped as we fell through the glass.

CHAPTER 9

Ariannah

§§

We were falling. My breath caught in my throat, so I couldn't scream, no matter how much I wanted to. I had brief glimpses of clouds and birds before a wave of rainbow colours engulfed us and we began to slow down.

"What's happening?" I managed to gasp to Rogue, praying she was still beside me.

"I don't know!" I heard her call back; her voice being blown away by the wind.

I started to feel lightheaded. Darkness slowly crept into the rainbow light, until it blocked it out completely, and I fell into unconsciousness.

§

When I awoke, I was lying on a soft mattress. I tried to sit up and found that I couldn't. "What's going on?" I gasped to myself.

"All is well," an unrecognisable voice whispered to me from somewhere to my left. "You and your sister fell far. Once it was in my power, I used my magic to cushion you. The effort affected you greatly. She has yet to wake."

"Where is she? Who are you? Why can't I move?" I asked erratically.

"She is beside you, on another bed. My name is Ariannah, and I am a healer. You cannot move due to the herbs that you have been given. This allows your entire body to heal before giving you control over your limbs. There are many who try to do too much before they are ready. The herb stops this impatience," the voice replied.

"Where are we?" I asked.

"You are among the Great Mountain Ranges," the voice went on. "My home is among the foothills." The owner of the voice stepped into view. Her eyes were almond shaped and a piercing green. Her hair was white blonde and fell over her tanned shoulders to her hips. Her ears, though curved at the tips, weren't sharp. As she turned to see to Rogue, I saw giant yellow and black butterfly wings that curved upwards out of her shoulder blades.

"You're a fairy?" I questioned, frowning, trying to blink away the confusion in my mind.

She paused. "No," she replied softly, turning back to me. "My father was an elf, my mother a sprite. Fairy wings are much different. Crossbreeding is not uncommon, but often frowned upon. My mother and father hid me from society for quite some time, fearing how I would be treated if people knew. I've been here almost my entire life." She turned and walked away. "You should be able to move now, should you wish to try."

I sat up gingerly. I was able to, but it was a lot harder than I expected. My bones felt like jelly and my muscles seemed to be arguing with my brain. As I tested out my arms, I noticed that Rogue was beginning to wake. "Ooooh… Where are we?" she groaned when she saw me.

"In Valeria," I hissed back. "We made it. We're in some mountains. Careful; you won't be able to move."

"Why not?" she squeaked, her eyes opening wide.

"You were given herbs that restrict movement to allow the body to heal," Ariannah interrupted.

"Who are you?" Rogue asked. "Who is she?"

"My name is Ariannah. Elven magic brought you to me for healing after your fall. You should gain your mobility back soon enough," she answered primly.

"Ranger; where are you?" Rogue whispered.

"I'm here," I replied, pulling myself off the bed and walking unsteadily over to her.

I gasped in shock and froze where I stood when I saw her face. "What is it?" Rogue questioned, panic in her voice.

"You've changed," I whispered. Her ears were sharper, and her eyes were rounder and darker. Her hair had turned a shocking pink, and visible on either side of her head were the tips of pale green wings. She was wearing what appeared to be a handmade dress, cut from some sort of plant that was a similar shade to her hair. Her feet were laced up to the knee in lavender purple flats.

Rogue started to throw her head from side to side in an attempt to see for herself, before looking up at me, surprise etched on her face. "So have you!" she gasped.

"Who are you?" Ariannah's voice cut in firmly. 'You have the look of a common fairy and elf, yet so alike that you must be sisters. You are both of, and not of, this world. I can tell. You're not from here yet belong here. Explain," she demanded, joining me by Rogue's bed, where she was struggling to sit up.

"We can't," I told her. Ariannah raised her eyebrows, her mouth in a hard line. I turned away and looked around the room in an attempt to avoid her gaze. It was a wooden house. The walls were covered in lush, green vines. Pots and pans hung from the ceiling and paintings covered the walls. The floor was dressed in a dark brown fur rug and there was a large stone dais in the centre of the room, with a small fire sitting underneath a large stone cauldron. I turned back to her. "I mean… we don't know how."

"Try," she said softly, danger in her voice.

"I don't suppose telling you we can't give you any information will be enough?" Rogue groaned again, finally sitting up.

"No," she said simply. We gave her a calculating look, before glancing at each other. "I can assure you, no matter what you have to tell me, it will never again leave my lips."

I took a deep breath. "Our ancestor?" I began slowly. "Romira Royce… created this world."

"Romira Royce?" Ariannah said, clutching her chest. She appeared deeply disturbed. Her face seemed to flicker in and out of focus. "Your ancestor?"

"You've heard of him?" Rogue asked. "Is he well known?"

"Well known?" she choked. "He is the creator! He is worshipped!" She looked at us incredulously, shaking her head in shock. "This isn't possible!"

"His son tried to take over the worlds his father had created and when his wife found out, she tried to stop him. Their names were Raphael and Raven," Rogue told her.

"I know the story well," Ariannah growled, before taking a deep breath and steadying herself. "They are our most ancient history! This world values truth above all else. We keep none of our past secret. All children in Valeria are taught our stories; knowledge is power."

"Sounds familiar," I smiled. "We were taught the same lesson."

Ariannah's face was dark and suspicious. "You expect me to believe you are the descendants of Romira Royce?"

"You said so yourself," I sighed. "We're not from here."

"But it is part of us," Rogue went on. "Raven went to great lengths to get us here and it wasn't for a holiday. What do you know?" Ariannah backed away, shaking her head, fear on her face. "What do you know?" Rogue repeated firmly as I helped her to her feet.

Ariannah turned away, her shoulders rising and falling as she took deep breaths. "Raven came here in a glow of golden light one evening in the time of Queen Irina," Ariannah started quietly. "She carried with her a pulsing stone. She pleaded to Queen Irina to keep the stone safe from the evil forces that sought to control it. Raven told her that Valeria needed the stone to protect it, as much as the stone needed protecting.

"The Queen agreed to have the stone taken care of, and entrusted it to her brother, Prince Lindon, who was henceforth known as the Guardian. The stone; the Heart of Valeria; turned pink, and from that moment Valeria changed. The Guardian found that, in his presence, no one could lie, and so the Heart of Valeria also came to be known as the Heart of Truth. This virtue is now carried by all Valerian citizens.

"When Raphael stormed the palace in Levindra, looking for Raven, the Guardian used the power of the Heart to dispel him," she continued. "After that, it became the custom for the Guardian to care for the Heart in a place of secrecy. When the new Guardian was to be appointed, they were led to the location for the transition, then they travelled to a new place of their choosing to begin their guardianship… and so the Heart of Truth has protected us ever since," she finished in almost a whisper. A hushed silence filled the room.

"Who is the Guardian now?" I asked her.

"She is an elven woman of twenty," Ariannah replied.

"That seems young," I responded. "How is the Guardian chosen?"

"Aren't elves immortal?" Rogue asked at the same time.

"That we are," she nodded. "Even a half breed one such as myself. The selection process is as unknown as the location. Only those wishing to be considered know what it ensues, and they are sworn to secrecy with the highest of magicks, and only the youngest elves are considered. This allows the Guardian to guard the Heart for hundreds of years.

"It is believed, by those in power, that giving it fewer transitions keeps the Heart strong, as it is sharing its power with fewer people. It is the same for the royal family. Our current Guardian is only the second to have the fortune of guarding the Heart of Valeria."

"Wait, hundreds of years?" Rogue repeated.

"Yes," Ariannah answered. "There are many who disagree with the decision, for only the elves are long lived, and this doesn't allow for those of other races to vie for the privilege of being Guardian. It has caused great unrest in the lands."

"There are other races?" I asked.

"Wait~" Rogue said, waving her hands around.

"~Yes there are four different races in Valeria~

"~GUYS!" Rogue yelled. We paused. She took a step towards Ariannah. "You said elven Guardians guard the Heart for hundreds of years and you've only had two?"

"Yes," Ariannah confirmed. "Why?"

I stared. "That's like eight *hundred* years." Rogue nodded.

"Yes," Ariannah repeated. "The year is 976, or 893 PH: post Heart."

"You're saying that in the three hundred or so years since Romira created in the worlds almost a thousand have passed here?" Rogue exclaimed.

"It's only been three hundred years?" Ariannah gasped. "Time must indeed move differently here."

"That means we have to get home as soon as possible. If we take too long our whole family could have aged and died before we get back!" I cried.

"Other way around," Rogue said. "Time is moving slower there, not faster."

I ignored her. "What is her name?"

"What?" Ariannah questioned. "Who?"

"The Guardian!" I cried. "What is her name?"

"I~ I do not know," Ariannah shrugged helplessly. "It was five years ago she was appointed, and it was only the shift in the land that alerted me to a new Guardian. It wasn't *announced.* Even the winds will not whisper her name for fear of her safety! The last Guardian would still be in possession of the Heart, were it not for a band of thieves having ambushed and slaughtered him in an attempt to claim it."

"What happened to them?" I asked.

"I'm guessing that he soon discovered it wasn't only the Guardian that protected the Heart?" Rogue questioned, looking from me to Ariannah.

"Aye, that they did," she agreed darkly, nodding.

"How do we find the Guardian?" I went on.

"Nobody knows where to find her," Ariannah insisted, before pursing her lips slightly in concentration. "But… the Guardian sends weekly missives to the Marble Palace reporting anything unusual."

"Wait," Rogue frowned. "If she's in hiding, how does she see things?"

"It's obviously the Heart!" I cut in. "Romira would've traveled all the lands he created. The Heart must allow the Guardians to see all over Valeria, but," I paused, turning back to Ariannah. "Does that mean she could already know we're here?"

"Perhaps," Ariannah said, raising her hands. "It is definitely possible."

"What's the Marble Palace?" Rogue interrupted.

"It is the home of the Royals. Romira chose Queen Ellennah and King Rajendra himself. A year after Romira left us for good, Princess Irina was born," she replied, with a sigh. "Her daughter, Eleria, rules us as Queen now, with her husband, King Evendon." Her face wrinkled in obvious displeasure. She clearly had no love for the King. "They have two children; Prince Fallon, who is no longer a child, but still very young by elven years; and Princess Elora, who was born only a few months ago. She will lead us next."

"How do we get there?" Rogue continued. Ariannah didn't answer. Instead, she stood up and crossed the room to a desk in the corner. She withdrew a large scroll out of the top drawer. The paper was aged and yellowing. She pulled at the red cord that bound it closed and unrolled it onto her long, wooden table. It was a map of Valeria.

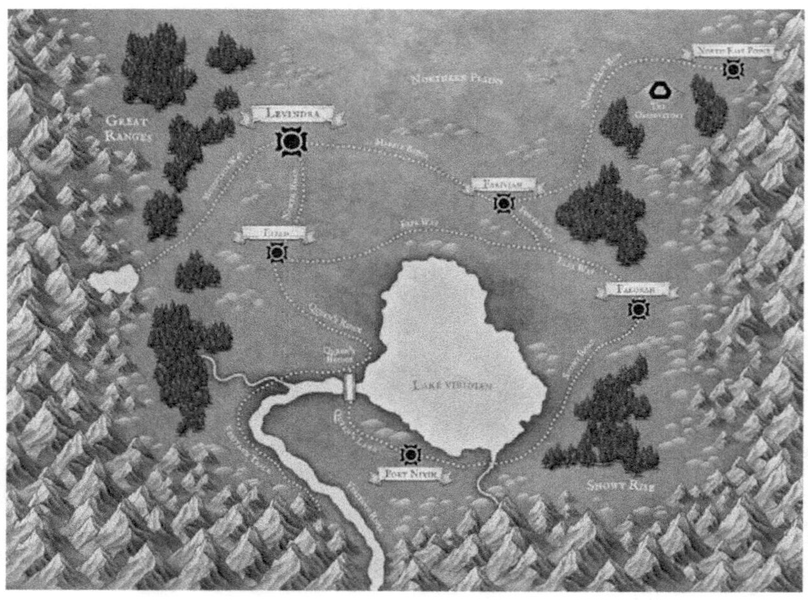

"We are here," she began to explain, pointing at the base of mountains near a small pool on the left of the map. "On the edge of the mid north region of the Valeria Mountain

Ranges. Just through the trees is a path that leads to this road, Mountain Way. Once you've joined the road," she continued, running her finger along the line that marked Mountain Way. "You follow it all the way to Levindra, the Capitol, where you'll find the Queen." She tapped a large sun shape at the top of the map.

"How long will it take to get there?" Rogue wondered.

She studied the map for a moment. "Based on standard travel, close to a week," she answered, before looking back to Rogue and me, "But with my magic winds speeding your way… you'll arrive by sundown tomorrow."

CHAPTER 10

Levindra

§§

The midday sun was beating down on us, as elven magic sped us towards the city of the royals. It was surreal; to have no wings, yet be flying, to have no power of my own, but being caught up in the wind and pulled along by forces far beyond me.

While we flew through the air like hawks, I thought over what had happened the night before. While we were planning and packing for the journey, a mirror in the corner of the room caught my eye. It had been there that I first caught sight of the new me. My eyes curved down at my nose and up at the outer edge and were now a blazing green. My ears had lengthened and curved into a sharp point. My skin had paled even further if that was even possible, and all my freckles and moles were gone. My hair was the darkest black, with blood red streaks running from root to tip. I was wearing dark brown leather pants and a tan cotton short sleeved shirt. Black boots covered my feet.

That wasn't all. In my shock, I had turned back to Rogue, and while I was looking at her, I thought about how I would look as a fairy; just for a second. I almost cried out when I looked back to the mirror. My roots were turning bright green, and as I watched, the colour flew down the rest of my hair as it started to shorten and curl. My eyes stayed green but turned two shades darker, and my ears curved slightly. My lips had turned pale pink, and when I looked down, I was no longer in brown leather, but a lime green dress that appeared to be made out of a type of leaf. My shoes laced up my calves like Rogue's, but were a dark, royal blue.

"What's going on?" I hissed to Ariannah in shock. This caught Rogue's attention. Her jaw dropped.

Ariannah frowned. "I think it is safe to assume," she began slowly. "That when you travelled to our world, it changed you to ensure that you could blend in. It should allow you to move easily among the races of Valeria." I gave her a dumbstruck look. Ariannah nodded to me. "You began thinking about fairies; you became one," she stated matter of factly, writing on a scroll rapidly, taking notes.

I came back to the moment, watching as the last of the Great Ranges on our left disappeared from view. How was that possible? I began thinking to myself, as we left the Great Ranges far behind. The magic of this place had changed us.

"Did she seem odd to you?" Rogue called to me over the sound of the wind. She seemed perturbed.

"Everyone seems odd to me," I yelled back. "Why?"

"She barely questioned what was happening! How often do random people just magically fall into your house for it to not faze you anymore?"

"We don't know how this world works! For all we know it's a lot more common than we realise!" Rogue maintained a concerned silence.

As the sun began to disappear behind the Ranges, I spotted a mound on the horizon. "What is that?" I called out. Rogue only shook her head in response. The closer we got, the more we began to see, and as we watched over the following minutes, more details finally revealed a great city surrounded by a wall, glowing in the slowly setting sun

"It's beautiful," Rogue breathed.

Within the hour, the magic of the winds died down and we landed a foot from the open gates. Vines worthy of Jack the Giant Slayer climbed twelve feet into the air, creating a large archway wide enough for ten people to walk through side by side. The vines continued on either side of the open archway and disappeared into the distance.

"Flying is great and all that, but it worries me a bit," I shivered, unsteady on my feet.

"I think it's incredible," Rogue grinned, hovering slightly with her shimmering wings.

"State your business," a fairy guard growled, stepping out from the side of the arch. He was a large bronze man holding a spear in one hand a shield in the other. His wings were steel grey and moth like and his eyes were beady and black.

"Uh. Um," Rogue stammered. "We- we're-"

"-We're visiting family," I stepped in.

"Yes!" Rogue exhaled. "Visiting family!"

He looked us up and down suspiciously before another guard stepped in. "Just let them through, Fabian!" she chided. She was a tall, lean elf with a scarf covering her hair. She had skin like coal and eyes that gave off just as much warmth as she smiled at us, before turning back to Fabian the fairy guard "No one of their description is on the watch list!"

"Watch list?" I repeated.

"Anyone could be an enemy, Vahla!" he shot back. "After the threats, the Capitol has received we cannot afford to be lenient!"

"No, we can't," she agreed with a sigh. "But that doesn't mean we can give everyone a hard time for travelling to the city. Let them pass," she ordered.

Fabian gave us one last glare, before standing aside to let us through. We stepped delicately the rest of the way around him and strode through the gates, forcing ourselves to walk slowly and calmly.

"Phew," Rogue breathed. "That was close."

"Yeah," I agreed. "I wonder why he was so wound up? And what exactly are the threats he was talking about? What watch list?"

"No idea," she huffed. "Just be glad we don't look like anybody on it."

As we travelled in the twilight, all thoughts of threats and watch lists were torn from my mind. The city was breathtaking. The vines continued throughout the city, but not in a way that made it seem unkempt or messy. They created walkway railings and decorated the more formal buildings, which were made of a smooth, brown stone.

The less formal buildings weren't buildings at all. They were the vines themselves, or, more often than not, large trees that twisted and curved to create houses, almost like they were grown for the purpose.

The largest trees held several families. The lower sections of the trees had thick, sturdy branches grown into a staircase that spiralled up into the canopy. Small children could be seen through the open tree knots that acted as windows. Through the canopy there were almost a dozen small, winged creatures flitting about the upper branches, disappearing in and out of topmost leaves.

"This is incredible!" I gasped. "It's like the entire city just grew out of the ground!"

"Shh!" Rogue said in a panicked whisper. "We're supposed to know this place!"

"Right," I nodded, adopting a less tourist like demeanour.

"How do we find the palace?" she asked out of the corner of her mouth.

"It'll be right in the middle of the city."

"How do you know?"

"Palaces always are."

"Yeah," she laughed. "In fantasy stories!"

"And what would you call this?" I whispered with a smile. We started laughing. I was shocked when it hit me how long it had been since the last time we'd laughed… really laughed. I fell silent as we walked down the winding paths of the Capitol.

I was right in thinking that the Marble Palace was at the city's centre. The large pathway we had followed from the main gates led straight to it.

As we threaded our way through the city, we noticed that while the outside edges homes were simple, the further in we went, the grander they became. The trees began to clear and we started to see more of the sky, the path turned from pale green grass to deep green moss, softer than any ground I'd ever felt under my feet before.

Like the entry into the city, the gateway into the Marble Palace was a large archway, true to its name; solid marble. There was not a single join in the entire archway. It was a masterpiece.

From the archway, we could see that to both the left and the right, there were more entryways into the Palace, none of them with gates, and while there were walls connecting each of the archways, they were low enough to climb over. While the palace was completely open, it was obvious that it had its own protection. "There's no way anyone can just walk in, right?" Rogue echoed my thoughts.

"We're about to find out," I replied. We walked through the archway and onto the palace grounds. The same soft moss covered the ground, and all over, there were small tufts of flowers or mushrooms.

The Marble Palace was magnificent. I had to tilt my head so far back that my neck ached to see the tops of the towers. Every inch was the same solid marble as the archways, again, all in one single piece. The main doors stood wide open, at the top of a tall, white marble staircase, leading from the palace lawns.

We climbed the staircase, far more breathless than we would have liked by the time we reached the top. Once through the open doors, we followed the throng of people into the large main corridor, all of whom seemed to be waiting for an audience with the King and Queen.

While most of them were elves, we could also see fairies, as well as a few smaller creatures with large butterfly wings like Ariannah's which must have been sprites, and tiny, flying, glowing creatures. As they milled around, a few official looking elves in uniforms walked around with scrolls, writing down notes as they spoke to each of the attendees, before directing them to their assigned place to wait. Large guards stood at attention along the walls on both sides of the corridor, spears and shields in their hands, ready to act at the first sign of danger.

"Everyone seems on edge, don't they?" I asked.

"Yeah," Rogue responded, casting a furtive glance around the room. "Something must have happened."

"Like what the main gate guards were saying… the threats," I whispered.

"Should we be elves or fairies? Do you think that the King and Queen will be biased towards their own kind?" Rogue asked.

"I don't know. Surely Romira wouldn't have chosen them if that was the case."

"But he didn't choose them. He chose the Queen's grand-mother," she reminded me as we joined the queue. "There's no way of knowing what she'll be like."

We hadn't been waiting longer than three seconds when we were approached by a short woman with spiky white hair and purple skin. "The Queen wishes to see you in private," she whispered to us, her violet eyes bulging.

"What?" Rogue asked, frowning.

"How?" I responded at the same time.

"Not here!" she hissed, gesturing for us the follow her as she turned on her heels and started walking briskly through the crowd. We looked at each other and shook our heads. Having no answers, we followed her. Every now and then, she'd glance back at us, for what reason we didn't know.

After a few moments, I couldn't keep silent any longer. "You're fairly short for an elf," I finally burst out.

"Well, I should say so!" she exclaimed, obviously insulted. "Can you not see that I'm a sprite, not an elf?"

"Oh," I mumbled, going quiet, noticing that her pink 'coat' was actually two butterfly wings folded around her. We followed her to the front of the queue and slipped through the large stone doors.

"Who are you?" a booming voice rang throughout the hall before the doors had the chance to close.

I looked toward the voice. At the far end of the room was a traditional dais, upon which sat three vine woven thrones. Sitting in the largest of the three was a smooth faced elf with dark brown eyes and deep purple hair that flowed over her burgundy gown and fell to her feet.

On top of her head sat a wreath style crown made of thin, delicate vines. Queen Eleria. She stood up from the throne and started down the stairs. "I sensed your presence the moment you reached my city. There is much for you to explain."

I stepped forward with Rogue beside me and we stopped at the foot of the stairs where we were met by the Queen, who was significantly taller than she looked from afar once we were up close.

Still on his throne sat King Evendon, a tall, pale elf with a vine circlet on his brow, his bright blue eyes shining. "We are not from here," I began.

"That," the Queen cut in. "We already know. Where did you come from and how did you come to be here?"

"It's a little hard to explain~" I started.

"~There was a mirror~"

"~We had to come through it to get here~"

"~We wouldn't be here if it wasn't important~"

"~We~"

"~We're the descendants of Romira Royce," Rogue finally spat out.

A lot happened all at once. The King got up from his throne and almost ran down the stairs to join the Queen. Queen Eleria turned to the sprite who led us in. "Leave us! We are not to be disturbed! Inform the staff!"

"Yes, Your Majesty!" she trilled, half running, half flying from the room.

Queen Eleria turned back to us. "Follow me," she ordered, turning on her heels and disappearing down a small passage to the left of the throne dais. The King, Rogue, and I followed, Rogue and I less easily given we were physically smaller and had no idea where we were going. We saw the Queen's dress disappear into a room on the right and when we crossed the threshold, we were in a room covered in a plush, white feathered rug that contained a chair… and a baby's crib. "Leave," she whispered to the three small, coloured lights that were floating above the crib. When the multi coloured balls drifted out of the room, the Queen turned back to us. "These are not your true forms," she murmured.

"No, they're not. When we got here, I was an elf and Rogue was a fairy. We don't know how to change back," I explained.

"We tried to turn back, but whatever magic this is, it won't let us," Rogue went on.

The royals froze for what felt like an eternity. "Rogue?" the King said finally, looking at her. He then turned to me "And Ranger?"

CHAPTER 11

Elora

§§

"You are Rogue and Ranger… of Raven's prophecy?" King Evendon demanded to know, more forcefully this time.

"We've never heard of this prophecy," Rogue told the royals. "But we are Rogue and Ranger."

The Queen leaned forward over the crib. When she straightened again, she was holding a baby in a soft, white silken gown. The baby burbled in its sleep, turning towards its mother's side. Under the black hair, a tiny, pointed ear could be seen.

"When Raven came here," she began, rocking back and forth with her baby. "It was 200 years after Romira had named my grandmother Queen. My mother had recently been crowned when she came, carrying the Heart of Valeria; of truth. It was given to my uncle, who became the first Guardian. Before she left, she claimed that one day, a Rogue and a Ranger would come for the Heart."

"She made a prophecy about us?" I questioned.

"Yes," the Queen nodded. "And you'll have to forgive our scepticism, but we are not going to allow you to seek the Guardian without proof of who you are, not with everything currently happening in my realm… and not after what happened to my uncle," she finished solemnly.

"What is this everything?" I asked. "We heard the guards talking at the gates about threats and a watch list? What's going on?"

The King and Queen looked at each other darkly. "There have been threats made by certain groups who are not pleased with the current governing structure of Valeria," the King explained vaguely.

"What do you mean?" Rogue pressed.

"There are those who believe it is wrong to inherit power; that it should be earned; that I should not be Queen," Queen Eleria continued, a sombre expression on her face, as she gazed at her sleeping baby. "They say it is discriminatory."

"How?" I asked, confused.

"All of the leaders would be elves," Rogue whispered, a look of dawning realisation on her face. "If the crown is inherited, then only elves would ever rule! Ariannah said cross breeding wasn't really accepted. So, the other races feel ignored?" she asked Queen Eleria and King Evendon.

"Yes. They feel elven leaders cannot legitimately rule them in a fair manner and ensure the needs of all of Valeria are met. They say we are biased toward our own kind," her voice broke slightly. "I have received threats, against me… and Elora," she stroked her baby's face.

The King's face was mutinous. "Rebels have threatened the lives of my wife and child, believing if they end the family line, there will be no one to replace them. The guards surrounding the city and palace have tripled in the past month."

"As Queen, all decisions for Valeria are yours?" I asked Queen Eleria, biting my lip.

"Yes," she answered, sniffing slightly. "Why?"

"Well… your people are feeling like they're not being heard. Maybe, if you let them in on the decision making process, they would feel more involved," Rogue suggested.

"Our people are being heard," the King snapped. "It is the other races that have the problem!"

"But, Your Majesty," I interjected. "As King and Queen, are not all of Valeria's people, elves or otherwise, your people?"

King Evendon looked shocked as though he had never before considered the idea, then angry at my interference. He looked to his wife, pensive and cautious. It was clear; change did not come easily to the King. I chalked it up to the longevity of the elves.

"Yes, well, there is much to consider," the Queen said, settling the baby back into her crib. "Once the security risk has been dealt with, of course. For now, we must get you on your way. So tell me, why should we believe what you say?"

"How can we prove who we are?" Rogue asked desperately.

"Easily," I said, stepping forward and focusing on my elven form. My body tingled all over, giving me goosebumps. When the sensation abated, the King and Queen were frozen, a stunned look on their angled faces.

"Well," Queen Eleria breathed. "That answers that."

"Surely we cannot trust them at face value?" the King interrupted, getting agitated at being disregarded.

"Yes… I believe we can," she said, coming closer to further analyse my face. "But if it will assuage your fear, husband; what were the words Romira spoke to each of the leaders of his Seven Worlds?" she suddenly asked.

"No idea~" I answered bluntly, raising my hands and dropping them back down to my sides.

"~The light need not be bright, to shine through the darkest night!" Rogue said quickly. The King gasped, recognising Romira's words.

"Mother? Father?" a deep voice called softly. A tall, dark haired elf with a silver circlet above his blue eyes came through the doorway. The spitting image of his father, this had to be Prince Fallon. "What is happening, Mother?" he asked her, frowning. "Ayvar told me you've paused all meetings?"

"My son," she started, crossing the room in two steps. "Summon Ford and Evanna, immediately." He nodded and disappeared back down the hallway.

"Come with me," Queen Eleria ordered, following her son out of the room, her husband at her heels.

"Who are Ford and Evanna?" I asked, casting a questioning glance at the King as we followed them down the hallway, struggling to keep up. The King remained resolute and seemed somewhat unhappy with current circumstances.

We joined Prince Fallon in a room towards the end of the hallway. Inside it was one thing; a giant mirror. It had a vined gilded frame that curled around in a spiral pattern.

"The mirror!" Rogue hissed to me, grabbing my arm. I shook her off.

"No," I whispered back, as the Queen approached it. "Romira obviously taught these people how mirrors could be used for transportation," I replied, more to myself than her. "It couldn't be our mirror."

Prince Fallon placed the mirror against the far wall, then closed his eyes and raised his hands. The mirror began to ripple and when it stopped, three people were stepping out of it. The first was a short woman; a fairy, with long locks of blue hair that flowed over her shoulders. Her pale blue dress was tied up with a woven belt of grass and daisies.

The second was a large elven man, with broad shoulders and coal black skin. His long dark hair was in braids, and a red-bladed sword was sheathed at his side.

The last was a short, teenaged boy. His green wings protruded from his back in two spikes and his hair was a pale straw colour. His forest green jumpsuit was obviously hand made, and at his side was a sheathed dagger.

"Ford, Evanna, Fillipe," the King said slowly. "This is Rogue and Ranger." All three of them gasped, as well as the Prince. Ford stepped forward threateningly; hand on the hilt of his sword. He was starting to draw it from its sheath, when the fairy woman, Evanna, stepped in front of him and rested her hand on his.

"How do we know?" he asked, staring us down, but not drawing his sword any further. Looking at his elven figure, and without being able to stop myself, I felt my ears lengthen and hair tingle. Ford roared in shock and leapt back.

"Oh, my," Evanna gasped again, her hand on her chest.

"Whoa!" Fillipe exclaimed. "How did you do that?"

"Ah… Uh… We don't exactly know how it works," Rogue stuttered as Ford made a second attempt to draw his sword.

"They have proven themselves, Ford. Calm yourself," Queen Eleria ordered.

"Why do you change?" Evanna asked, interrupting the exchange with a wave of her hands.

"Ariannah told us that we are able to change so we can blend in," I explained. "But like Rogue said, we don't know exactly how or why it happens."

"Ariannah?" Prince Fallon repeated, seemingly alarmed as he looked quickly at his father. "Of the Great Ranges? How do you know her?"

"Yes," the King growled, fuming. "How do you know her? You seem to be consorting with many powerful people and now you're here for the Guardian's information? This is starting to seem very suspicious, especially given the threats we've received!"

"When we first arrived here, we woke up in Ariannah's home," I explained. "She took care of us and told us that if we needed to find the Guardian, coming here was how we'd do it. You all seem to know her well?" The Prince went bright red but nodded only slightly.

"How coincidental," the King replied, with a raised eyebrow. "Ariannah is a very powerful elf, and as such, will be a great ally in the coming war," he stated with a forceful look at his son. Prince Fallon's eyes dropped to the floor.

"Elven sprite," I corrected factually, thinking I was being helpful and once again being proven wrong by the gaze of the King's icy glare.

"Now is not the time to quibble over *meaningless* details," he said gruffly.

Before he could continue, Queen Eleria stepped in. "Rogue, Ranger, this is the Guardian Elva's family," she introduced. "They will help guide you to her and hopefully gain her favour in these trying times."

"Well," Evanna began, seemingly disturbed at being summoned only to have her daughter discussed as though she were a weapon. "We would hope that war would be the last resort. We certainly wouldn't want our daughter involved in such matters unless all of Valeria was at risk."

"Definitely not," Queen responded firmly. "War is absolutely not a consideration at this time." Her husband frowned, evidently unhappy at being overruled.

"So! Her name is Elva," I said in a desperately obvious attempt to change the mood. I met Ford's eyes. "Where do we find her?"

"You don't," he growled back. "After what happened to the last Guardian, whom I called Brother, and now having my daughter go against my wishes to become the new Guardian, I will not have her location released to anybody, especially at this time of civil unrest, where many would use the power she yields for their own purposes, or see it eradicated entirely."

"I'm sorry," Rogue responded, directing her gaze to Evanna. "We can't possibly understand what your family has experienced to have a daughter choose Guardianship, and we don't know anything about what's happening among the people. We only know that if we don't find Elva and the Heart, it's not just Valeria at stake," she explained, her voice wavering.

Ford's face didn't change as he looked to his wife. After a pause, he looked down and let his hand drop from his sword's hilt. Evanna came forward. "Are you really Rogue and Ranger? Of legend?"

"Yes," Rogue answered. "Our ancestor, Raven, sent us a message to collect the Heart and return it to the place she took it from. If we don't, your world faces far greater heartache than losing a daughter to Guardianship, or the royal family to a revolution."

Evanna pursed her lips, her face turning pale and frightened. As she opened her mouth to speak, a guard rushed into the room. "Your Majesty! The outer wall of the city has just been breached. There is a mob headed directly for the palace!" she said quickly. "You must flee, now!"

"What?" the Queen frowned. "Freya? What is this?"

"Sedition, Your Majesty!" Freya spat. "Treason! They mean to dethrone you!"

"This is not possible," the King said in a shocked whisper. "They cannot possibly get into the palace. The arches?"

"They remain intact, Your Majesty," Freya confirmed.

"What about them?" I asked.

"They protect us," Prince Fallon answered, resting his hands on his mother's shoulders. "No one meaning harm can get through them."

The moment unceremoniously ended when a second guard crashed into the room. "Your Majesties!" he gasped, struggling to catch his breath.

"Gregor! What is it, man?" the King yelled, shocked at the intrusion.

"THE BABY, YOUR MAJESTIES!" he bellowed. "PRINCESS ELORA HAS BEEN KIDNAPPED!"

CHAPTER 12
The Passage

§§

"WHAT?" Prince Fallon cried out, as the King started yelling incoherently and the Queen fled the room.

We all took off after her. "Your Majesty, WAIT! WE MUST PROTECT YOU!" Freya screamed after her. When we caught up to Queen Eleria, she was in a crumpled heap on the floor by her baby's crib, sobbing into a soft green baby blanket.

"Eleria!" the King barked, dropping down to his wife. "It is the rebels! I was expecting something like this! Do not fear; we will find her. I promise!"

"*She is gone!*" the Queen sobbed, her voice coming in short breaths. "They'll never- keep her *alive!* We *know*- why she- was taken!"

"Your Majesty," I said softly, stepping forward. "Rogue and I will find her," I said without thinking.

"What?" Rogue cut in.

"Yes," I nodded to her, before crouching down by the Queen. "We'll find Elora. We'll get her back to you."

The Queen peered up at me, her eyes red and puffy. "How?" she croaked.

"This is our family's world," I told her. "We're here because of what we can do. If we can reunite the Heart of Ventura surely we can find a baby," I reasoned.

"Your Majesty," Gregor warned. "The mob draws near. We have to get you out."

"But-" the Queen began.

"-Where?" I cut her off, standing and turning to face the guard. "How do we get out if the doors are being watched?"

"Uhh," he paused, looking around me to the Queen, still on the floor. She took another deep breath and hauled herself to her feet. She gave a single nod and Gregor looked back at me. "There are tunnels under the Marble Palace that lead to safe houses outside the city."

A third guard joined us in the room. This one was a small red glow. As I looked closer, I saw a small angular body and wings beating faster than a hummingbird's. "Your Majesty," they bowed. "The barriers have been breached. The traitors are in the palace."

"We need to leave," Freya said, raising her spear. "Now!"

I turned to Gregor. "Where is the closest tunnel?"

"The gates at the end of the corridor," he responded immediately.

"No," the Queen interrupted softly, crossing the room, her hands twisting around in the baby blanket. "There is no way anyone who wished us harm could have crossed through the archways, which means, either these people don't mean us any harm… or they were told about the tunnels."

Rogue groaned. "Then we have no safe way out?"

"We have one," a small voice whispered. We turned to the voice, standing at the other end of the room, by the crib. Fillipe. "The mirror," he whispered.

"They will follow us just as easily," Ford said in a deep voice.

"Not if we break the mirror," I responded, looking around the room at the shocked, incredulous faces. "Think about it. We go through, then break the mirror. They won't be able to follow."

"That mirror is priceless!" the King yelled in outrage.

"Is it worth more than your lives?" Rogue retorted. King Evendon shook his head and turned away. "We go through the mirror and destroy it once we're on the other side."

"They'll know where we've gone. If they can't follow us directly, the mirror's very existence on this end will still alert them to our location," Ford warned.

The hope in my chest died momentarily, before flaring back up. "We stay," I said quietly.

"I'm sorry, WHAT?" Rogue screeched.

"You all go through," I started. "We shatter the mirror once you're gone. Then, we get rid of the pieces," I went on.

"No one will know the mirror existed. As far as anyone can assume, you're in one of the tunnels."

"And what will you do?" Fillipe asked.

"Yes, Ranger, *what will we do?*" Rogue hissed through gritted teeth.

"Elora was only just taken," I answered, moving to the Queen and clasping her hands in mine. She still held the blanket. "She's here somewhere. We can blend in. No one knows us. We can find her if we stay!"

Rogue deflated, looking downcast. The Queen's face changed from devastated, to not quite excited, but close. "We stay and we find the baby," Rogue said, eyes drifting. "And hope we make it out alive."

§

One by one, the royals, their guards, and the Guardian Elva's family passed through the mirror. Ford gave us a final glance before he nodded and stepped through. He had insisted on being the last to leave.

When he had fully disappeared and the mirror had stopped rippling, I slapped Rogue's arm and pointed to the frame. "Help me." We gripped the edge of the frame and pulled it off the wall, letting it fall to the ground with an earth shattering crash. I flinched.

"Ugh," Rogue cringed. "I hope nobody heard that."

"How do we get rid of it?" I whispered.

"I don't know! Magic?" Rogue suggested, waving her hands. "We're fairies, right?"

"Yes," I answered, looking at the broken remains of the mirror. "We are." I bit my lip in concentration and held my hands out to the pieces, willing them to disappear. "Help me!" I snapped at Rogue when nothing happened. She put her hands out with me. I felt a tingle begin in my fingertips. "Yes!" I gasped. "Keep going!" The pile of mirror and frame pieces burst into flames, causing Rogue and me to jump back, shrieking. "It'll do! RUN!" I ordered.

"*Fire?*" Rogue screamed as we fled from the room. "Is that what you were *trying* to do?"

"I WAS JUST TRYING TO GET RID OF IT! I DIDN'T CARE HOW!" I yelled back, running down the hallway.

There was a left turn at the end of the corridor. As I turned to follow it, Rogue stopped running. "Wait!" she called out.

"What? We can't stop! We just started a fire down there!" I squealed, panicked, as I hopped from one foot to the other, eager to keep going.

"Think, Ranger!" she demanded, dropping her voice. "Gregor said at the end of this corridor there was a tunnel entrance! We were with Elora minutes before she was taken! The Queen thinks someone leaked the tunnel secrets and if they did, this was the closest tunnel to Elora when she was kidnapped!"

I stopped moving. She was right. "How do we find it?" I asked softly.

Rogue started examining the walls, running her hands over the marble patterns and fiddling with the torch bracket hanging near the corner. As I joined her, I began to hear a rumble starting above us, with thumps and yelling. "Hurry," Rogue said. "We don't have a lot of time."

I nodded and started examining all the twists and whirls of the marble pattern on the connecting wall. My fingers followed the pale grey and pink patterns until I reached the corner of the corridor, where the wall Rogue was investigating met mine. "There's nothing here! We must be miss- ROGUE!" I gasped, pulling her towards the corner.

"What? What is it?"

"Look!" I ordered, pointing to the space where the two walls met. "Look at the groove!"

"Ranger," Rogue said in exasperation. "It's just the join where the walls meet."

"That aren't anywhere else in the entire palace!" I reminded her. "Or on any of the arches. All of the marble used to build the palace is a single piece!" Rogue's eyes widened in realisation. "There shouldn't be any grooves or joins anywhere. Push!" I threw myself at the wall with Rogue and we pushed with all the weight of our bodies. Nothing happened.

"Maybe there's a password?" Rogue huffed, looking up to the ceiling and down to the floor for more clues.

"We don't have time for passwords!" I cried. "Every moment we're stuck here, Elora gets further away!" I struck the wall in frustration and after a moment's pause, fell right through it.

"Ranger!"

I had fallen through and landed roughly on the other side. "I'm ok!" I yelled back, getting up off the dusty stone floor and brushing my hands clean on my clothes. "It's ok, come through!"

"I can't! The wall won't let me! What did you do?"

"Nothing! I just said we needed to get to Elora!"

"Elora?" she repeated softly before her body appeared on my side of the wall. She caught herself before she fell. "We found the password," she said flatly.

"Hopefully, we find her just as easily," I responded. I gave a swift nod, turned on my heels, and started running along the dark tunnel.

The walls were made from the same marble as the palace, but the floors were rough cobblestone. Large stone torches glowed softly along the tunnel, illuminating the passage; just enough to see as we ran. The passage twisted and turned often, and we were forced to slow down when the incline started to rise. We had to stop altogether, hearts pounding in our chest when it levelled out and the floor disappeared entirely.

"Who left that staircase here," I groaned, rolling my ankle on the first step before Rogue could catch me from falling down the entire flight.

"No time for that," Rogue said bluntly, urging me on. "We need to keep moving. Guaranteed there'll be scouts checking this tunnel as soon as they realise the royals are gone." We pushed on, down the stairs, further along the passage. Hours passed. We only ever rested by walking, never stopping altogether.

As the eternal night continued, our stomachs growled, our throats were parched and our feet ached. Still, we forced ourselves onward, only pausing when the air began to feel moist and we noticed water seeping up through the floor. "What is this?" I questioned, as a low rumble started above us. "Are we under the lake?"

Rogue looked concerned, her brow furrowed as she gazed at the ceiling. "We couldn't possibly be that close to Lake Viridian, and that wouldn't explain the noise," she breathed softly.

"Is that... a water pump?" I asked incredulously, following her gaze. "Are we under a city?"

"That doesn't make sense!" she said, perturbed. "The closest city was a week away without magic!"

"Maybe there are towns not on Ariannah's map?"

"Maybe," she agreed. "One way to find out." We headed further down the tunnel with renewed vigour, anxious to get out of the passage. As we ran, the pounding in my head and the breath heaving from my chest blocked everything out.

The closer we came to our destination, wherever it was, the more the grinding, rumbling sound overpowered them, until I couldn't hear them anymore. It soon began to sound like it was all around us and it became harder to run as the rumbling shook the ground beneath our feet.

"I sure hope these tunnels are reinforced!" Rogue yelled over the din. I said nothing, but pushed on, desperate to get out of the damp, musty air and into the light. I was starting to feel dizzy.

"There!" I cried out. Finally, there was a pinprick of glowing light at the end of the tunnel. I started to sprint, feeling a cool breeze on my face. "Yes!" I gasped as I exploded out of the tunnel and into a wooded glade. In the shade of an ancient lilting willow, I dropped to the ground and ran my hands through the lush green grass, trying to ground myself after feeling elevated for so long. "Breathe," I whispered to myself. "Just breathe."

"Well, this is definitely an improvement," Rogue panted, sitting on the grass beside me. "I wish we'd known how long those tunnels were before we decided to use them. You ok?"

I nodded, eyes still closed, breathing heavily. "We didn't have much of a choice. This was our only lead to Elora," I puffed, struggling to catch my breath, coughing a little. "How long were we down there, do you think?"

"All night," she answered, crossing the glade to the edge of the trees. "The sun's well and truly risen. Must be almost noon."

"I'm starving," I announced as my heart began to settle, the buzzing in my head lessened and I felt my stomach growl. "We need to eat."

"Well, that should be easy enough," she said. "Come and see." She pointed as I joined her at the tree line, where a tall stone pillar could be seen in the distance. "That's definitely not a town."

CHAPTER 13

Farivian

§§

This city was different from the Capitol. Instead of the rich mahoganies, deep red rosewoods, and almost black walnuts, the houses and buildings were all light and honeyed oaks, ashes, and maples. The trees sometimes grew in groups, but even where they didn't, the branches all interlocked so thickly that in places, the sun couldn't shine through. In these darker, quieter areas of the city, the air was cooler and damper and mushrooms and toadstools littered the cold ground, lighting up the paths; with either magic or biology, I didn't know.

There was no stone for the paths; no marble for their official buildings; only trees, grassy mounds, and hidden caves. It was as though nature itself had grown to create the lives of its people, rather than the citizens using nature's resources to create their lives. It was awe inspiring.

"Excuse me?" I asked a sprite as he flew past. I never did grasp how such large stout bodies could be held up by wings.

I shook my head slightly to rid myself of the thought before I could picture him falling from the sky and start to laugh. "Um, we were meant to meet our aunt here for lunch but can't find the place she told us to go to. Can you help us?"

"Why certainly!" he replied in a chipper voice. "Not familiar with Farivian, are we?"

"No sir," Rogue answered, continuing quickly, in sync with me. "We were visiting and just arrived here in… Farivian. We've never been here before."

"No trouble at all, no trouble at all!" he trilled. "Now, if your aunt planned a lunch I can only assume she's expecting to meet you at the Lookout Tavern! Best place in the city. Excellent food!"

"Thank you!" I replied. "Yes, that sounds right. Where would we find it?"

"City centre!" he pointed back along the path he had come from. "Can't miss it!"

"Thank you again!" Rogue called as he flew away and we turned to follow his path. As soon as he was out of sight, she looked at me. "You can just pull them from anywhere, can't you?" I smirked.

§

"Lookout Tavern," I read, as we crossed the main city court-yard. "Not bad."

"Not bad at all," Rogue agreed, nodding.

The Lookout Tavern was several large maple trees all growing together. Further up near the branches we could see staircases winding up and down the trunks, leading to different coloured wooden doors. Inside, the maple trees were hollow. Growing out of the floor were a few dozen tables with small stools surrounding them. On the far wall of the Tavern was a long wooden ledge, which acted as the bar, and behind which stood a sprite barman and a fairy barmaid. At the very end was a large serving window, where several cooks were delivering meals to the wait staff.

"Yeeesssss!" I groaned, taking the nearest seat and grabbing a menu.

"Take it easy," Rogue said softly as she gingerly took a seat beside me. "We need to draw as little attention as possible. I nodded in agreement as I examined the menu.

Within seconds a blue pixie in a tiny uniform and matching sized notepad and pencil appeared at our table. "Afternoon ladies!" she squeaked. "Drinks to start?" I stared, forcing myself not to say anything, knowing I was going bright red with a dumb look on my face.

"Uhh yes!" Rogue took over, kicking me underneath the table. "As much water as you can fit on this table, please. We are very thirsty; we've travelled a long way."

"Is that so?" she said. "Well, we'll get you sorted in no time! Back in a flash!" And quite literally, there was a flash of light and she was gone.

"Ohhhhhh wasn't she the most adorable thing you've ever seen?" I squealed in the loudest whisper I dared. "In her teeny little uniform and teeny little apron!"

"*Shhh!*" Rogue admonished. "Stop or you'll have us found out!" I breathed in deeply in an attempt to compose myself, committed to regaining control before the pixie came back with our drinks.

"How is she even going to get it here?" I asked, confused. "It's bound to be more than she can carry." In that instant, two large pitchers appeared on our table with two matching glasses.

"Question asked and answered!" Rogue replied, happily grabbing a glass and a pitcher.

"Well, hello girls. How interesting that we would meet again," a lilting voice said suddenly. "I thought you were headed for the Marble Palace?"

Ariannah was wearing a long red cloak with the hood drawn back. "Hi! What are you doing here? I thought you said you didn't leave your home?" I asked, shocked to see her.

"I said my parents kept me hidden away most of my life." She corrected, aloof. "But now I am an adult who can make her own decisions and my parents are no longer around to dictate them," she said rather proudly. "I frequent the Tavern when I'm in town meeting with the merchants who carry the supplies I need for my healing balms and solutions," she explained. What brings you here?"

Neither of us knew what was and wasn't safe to say. That was new; usually, it was just me. "We came across the Prince on a hunting trip," I lied. "He said they hadn't heard from the Guardian in months and that we should seek her family directly. Apparently, this was the best place to start, but we've decided to stop for the night."

Ariannah looked annoyed. "I wouldn't take Prince Fallon at face value," she sneered. "He is a rather pompous and arrogant boy, much like his father. You need to go and see the Queen. The Capitol is where you need to be. I can feel it," she insisted.

I was thrown by her description of Fallon. He had seemed the very opposite when we had met him, and clearly, she hadn't heard of the attack on Levindra, or surely she wouldn't be insisting on our return. But is it possible she senses we need to be there *because* of the uprising?

"Maybe you're right," Rogue replied, filling her cup again. "We'll head back first thing in the morning. The Guardian family clearly aren't here anyway."

Ariannah nodded approvingly. "Very good. Just because Valeria values honesty above all else, that doesn't mean we aren't prone to misinformation because we asked a less than ideal source!" With a final nod, she stood up. "Have a good evening girls." And just like that, she was gone as quickly as she'd appeared.

"That was weird," Rogue said. "Is it bad that we lie so easily in a world that expects honesty?"

"Probably," I sighed as the pixie returned to take our order. "But you have to admit, it gives us an edge."

"Excuse me, Miss?" Rogue asked her. "The doors above us? What are they for?"

"Hyx!" she answered, "My name is Hyx! They are our rooms and apartments. We are a fully serviced hotel as well as a tavern! Are you girls looking for somewhere to stay?"

"Yes, we are," I told her. "Are there any availabilities tonight?"

"Oh, there are always vacancies dear!" she replied. "Maples are such sweethearts! They'd never turn anyone away! If we run out of rooms, they simply make more!"

I stared blankly at her, as my mind tripped over itself trying to understand exactly what she'd told me. "That's very nice of them!" Rogue cut in as she pulled out the coin bag from beside the map Ariannah had given us. She dumped a heap of coins on the table for the room and our meals. Hyx's eyes widened slightly, but she waved her hands and the coins disappeared.

"Come with me!" she piped, flying out of one of the knots in the tree behind the bar. We followed her through it and found ourselves in an outdoor eating area. Fruit trees of all varieties had root systems growing up and out of the ground in arches, providing tables and chairs to outdoor diners. We followed her around the edge of one of the maples until the seating disappeared and a large apple tree came into view. Its trunk was split in two to create a walkway into a private area that had small, bubbling pools.

"These are the hot springs. They act as our bathhouse. Please be respectful of our other lodgers. Over here is the first staircase, but of course, being fairies you won't need them! It will be much faster if we fly!"

I stopped short. "Uh oh," I whispered.

"Is everything alright?" Hyx asked when she saw that I'd stopped.

"Yes, of course!" Rogue answered for me. "She just had a rough time on her last flight."

"Oh?" Hyx said inquiringly.

"Storms," Rogue said quickly. "She'll be ok. You'll be ok." She took my hand and squeezed it, then pulled me into the sky. I wanted to close my eyes but forced myself to keep them open and on the blue glow in front of me. I fumbled a few times but got the hang of it eventually. I certainly did not appreciate flying the way Rogue did.

About a third of the way up one of the towering maples, a pale pink door opened and Hyx flew in, landing neatly on a table in the entryway. "Oh, this is lovely!" she exclaimed, looking around with interest.

"You've never seen inside before?" I asked breathlessly as I stumbled through the doorway.

"Oh, of course!" she giggled. "But each room is different, you see? The maples know what you need and they provide accordingly!

"Well, hit the buzzer if you need anything! Room service menu and tourist brochures are over here on the wall," she directed, pointing above her to the racks, next to which was a dark brown tree knot.

"Hyx, what is that?" Rogue suddenly asked, pointing back out the door, where the tall pillar Rogue had first seen on our arrival could be seen in the distance.

"That's the Observatory," Hyx answered, before seeing our confused face. "Where the study of the stars' constellations and alignment takes place?"

"Oh yes! Of course!" I laughed nervously. "I just never dreamed it was so big!"

"It needs to be! There are professionals who study all their lives to be able to read the prophecies, so it houses much of the north eastern population!" She pulled a brochure off the wall and handed it to me. "It's well worth the visit if you have the time! Have a good evening!" She flew out of the door and it closed politely behind her.

I nodded in awe, my mouth hanging open as I gazed up at the wood of the maple tree that formed the ceiling of our room. "We definitely don't give trees enough credit," I mumbled, more to myself than Rogue, running my fingers along walls. The leaves outside seemed to rustle bashfully at the recognition.

The room had all wooden furniture growing out of the floor, just like the tables and chairs down in the restaurant, and soft, green, leafy cushions and linens covered the lounge and beds. Flowered curtains; vines and flowers woven together; hung from the open tree knots.

"We need to sleep," Rogue said, rubbing her eyes. "Help me close the windows." As she made to pull the curtains closed, there was another soft rustling and the windows and curtains slowly closed themselves before a creaking sound filled the room and darkness descended all around us. When we peeked around the curtains, we saw that several branches had covered the windows to block out the light. "Thanks, Maple," Rogue whispered, as we climbed into bed and fell asleep.

CHAPTER 14

The Stolen Princess

§§

When I awoke Rogue was already up. "What time is it?" I burbled sleepily.

"Sundown," she responded absentmindedly from the table.

"Wuzrong?" I grumbled, stretching.

"Just thinking. I have an idea."

"Yeah?"

"This is the main hotel in the city."

"Is it?"

"Yes, I checked," she pointed at the wall of brochures Hyx had shown us. "And we think that whoever took Elora followed the same tunnel we did."

"You think whoever took her might be staying here too?" I questioned.

Rogue shook her head and shrugged. "Just as likely they have a hideout somewhere in the city."

"We need to look around; see if anyone showed up with a baby today!"

"How? You think the maples will help us burglarise themselves?"

"I don't think that would count as burglary if the owners were helping us do it," I muttered.

Suddenly, there was a rustling at the window and when Rogue went and opened it, a long thin branch slinked inside and hit the buzzer for room service. "What in the maple?" On its way out the branch dragged itself across the wall and a sheet of paper fell off the noticeboard that held the brochures.

"Help wanted," Rogue whispered, a smile growing on her face. "If you are keen and reliable with strong attention to detail, then look no further than the Lookout Tavern for employment! Currently hiring maids and wait staff! THIS IS IT!"

"Maple!" I cheered before a voice cut me off.

"Hello?" a gruff voice called. It was coming from a pink tulip hanging out of the wall next to the buzzer. "Concierge; how can we help?"

"HI!" Rogue called cheerfully in her best customer service voice. "We saw that you are looking to hire maids and waitstaff and my sister, and I are very interested. We're new to the city and have housekeeping experience!"

"We do?" I asked.

"-Shh!" she hissed back.

"Wonderful!" the deep voice responded. "Are you able to meet the Head of Housekeeping in the restaurant?"

"Yes, of course! We'll be right down!" she answered excitedly.

Too excited and overwhelmed at the thought of finding the baby Princess to care about the heights, I threw myself out of the tree and we flew down to the back entrance of the restaurant, walking inside as calmly as we could and taking a seat at the bar. We had to make sure we made a good impression. A chance like this wouldn't present itself again.

"Good evening ladies," the barman greeted us warmly. The dinner shift barman was a tall elven man with long green hair tied back into a neat ponytail. "What can I get for you?"

"Tea please," Rogue answered. I was still rather green from the flight and wasn't willing to risk talking. "And if you see the Head Housekeeper, could you please let them know we're here? They're expecting us."

The barman gave a gracious nod and disappeared through the service door. "What's the plan?" I asked, hand still over my chest as my stomach churned.

"We get the jobs and use our access to snoop," Rogue answered plainly. "Obviously."

"Obviously," I repeated blankly. "Nothing could possibly go wrong there."

"Well, you were right about one thing," she murmured. "It's not burglary if the owner is helping you."

"Inah; your visitors," the barman announced, returning with a sprite woman in a bright orange rose petal dress and curly yellow hair. The barman also carried a tray with a teapot and two crystal cups and saucers.

"You are the guests interested in the cleaning work?" she asked, leaning over the bar and very obviously sizing us up. "Do you have experience?"

"Yes mam," I answered. "We were part of a household responsible for the maintenance of a castle! Your ad mentioned strong attention to detail and we most certainly have it!"

"A castle?" she repeated, a look of confusion on her face. "Interesting. Where? Not the Marble Palace?"

"Oh no," Rogue continued. "Nothing so extravagant. There are some families who had them built further south, near the river." I was impressed at how easily the lies rolled off her tongue. I guess I taught her well. Or Dad had. I remembered him fondly as the memory of him telling Uncle Reiner we'd signed the deed came back to me. I had to shake myself slightly to pull myself out of it to hear what Inah said next.

"*Elven* families, I presume?" she was muttering under her breath.

"Now, Inah, why would you presume that?" the barman questioned, clearly offended.

"It is well known the royal family placed those closest to them in positions of power; giving them allotments of land

and such. It's no secret!" she chided, glancing back to us with a meaningful look. "Just more elves that have the rest of us cleaning up after them." She hopped off the bar and headed to the service door. "Come with me girls!"

I gave the barman an apologetic look, before getting up and following Rogue around the bar and through the service door, where Inah was waiting, holding two pressed maids uniforms. "These should alter themselves to fit. Lilies have always been people pleasers."

"Thank you," we chorused, and went into the staff bath~ rooms to change.

"Perfect!" Inah declared upon our return. "Well, I will trial you on the sienna orange room. Head there in the morning when you wake up and when you're finished, I'll come to inspect. What room are you in tonight?" she asked.

"We're almost halfway up? The pale pink room?" Rogue answered.

"Ah yes! I went past it this afternoon. How are you liking it?"

"Oh, it's beautiful! The maples have been incredibly ac~ commodating." Rogue said.

"Except," I said quickly. "There was a lot of noise we could hear out of the window?" I told her.

"There was?" Rogue muttered.

"Yeah, you might have slept through it," I rushed on, waving her quiet. "There was a lot of banging and what sounded like crying?" Rogue's eyes widened slightly. "Does someone here… have a baby?"

"N-no?" Inah stammered, sounding shocked at the suggestion. "I don't believe so? I do all the room checks when they open for visitors and there haven't been any with cribs in them. The maples would never allow a child to go uncatered for!" she said with finality.

"No," I agreed, nodding, as my mind began to wander. "They definitely would not."

§

It was late. All the exterior hotel mushroom lights were emitting a soft green glow. The restaurant had long since closed and now only rowdy bar goers were left. We could hear the distant cheers of the local hunting club as they chanted their slogan over and over far below us.

Rogue and I were dressed in our uniforms. They would allow us into every room in the maples.

"We do a quick sweep to see if we can hear anything and if not, we check room by room, starting at the top and working our way down," I planned out loud as I pulled my dress tighter. "If someone is hiding the Princess here, they'd want to be as far away from the public as possible."

"Ok. I'll start on the eastern side and work my way back," Rogue agreed. "You start here and meet me in the middle.

"Got it." The door opened gently and we both rose into the sky. Rogue disappeared into the night, while I flew directly upward, circling the trunk and listening intently as I drifted slowly through the trees.

The night was cool and clear. Thousands of stars could be seen from the higher branches above the canopy of the city. It was silent. I couldn't hear a thing that could possibly lead me to Princess Elora.

After I'd made my way around the western maples, I met Rogue at the centre trunk. "Anything?" she asked.

"No," I replied, shaking my head desolately. I didn't know what else to do. "I really thought this would work."

"Hey, it still might," Rogue answered. "Let's start checking the rooms." I sighed deeply and followed her back to the top of the tallest of the maples, where we stopped at a dark blue door. "Housekeeping!" Rogue called softly, reaching for the knob; but there wasn't one.

"What? The uniforms should give us access, shouldn't they?" In response, a few of the branches above us have an ominous creak.

"The maples; they know. That's why they're not letting us in!" I hissed, thinking quickly. "The maples know… and they wouldn't let a baby go uncatered for." I flew up slightly, away from the dark blue door, and landed in a fork in the branches.

"What are you doing?" Rogue whispered, looking around to check for anyone who might see us.

"The maples know," I repeated, holding my hand out to the trunk and closing my eyes. "Lies and deception aren't going to work."

"Ok?" Rogue answered. "And?"

"Shh." I turned back to the tree. "There is a baby here," I said softly. "Do you understand me?" There was a rustling reply. "The baby was stolen." I pressed as much feeling into the word as I could. "She was taken from her family. She's scared and with someone who could hurt her if they haven't already. Please… help us," I urged, starting to cry in frustration.

The rustling stopped entirely as the maples appeared to freeze altogether. Rogue gasped. "Ranger!" My head snapped up to where she was pointing. All along the trunk of the next maple over, a line of glowing mushrooms shone slightly brighter than the rest and pulsed ever so slightly. My eyes followed the line of lights higher into the tree until they disappeared into the topmost branches.

I took off as fast as my wings could carry me, ducking quickly under the branches as Rogue struggled to keep up. "Ow!" she groaned, as she crashed headlong into me on the other side of the final branch, where I hovered in the air, completely still, staring at a dark green door as it silently opened.

We crept inside, stepping as delicately and deliberately as we could. A pale luminescence glowed at the far end of the room. "Cover me," I whispered, and as Rogue checked every corner of the small apartment, looking for any sign of a baby or anyone else, I made for the glow as quickly as I dared, my heart pounding in my chest.

When I reached it, it was just another of the mushroom night lights. I turned slowly on the spot, taking in every inch of the room. "Come on," I whispered into the darkness. "Where are you?" There was a desk in the corner covered with scrolls. One was laid out, held open with small stone paperweights.

"There's no one here," Rogue said as she joined me by the light. "The entire apartment is empty."

"Maybe whoever was here is downstairs enjoying the party?" I suggested with a frown. "Look at this map. Anything look familiar to you?" It was what looked like a massive maze of rooms and halls; a building blueprint.

Rogue studied the image for a moment. "It's the palace!" she gasped. "This is it!"

"Yes, but-" Before I could continue, there was a creak above us, from deep within the maple. "What is it? What are you trying to say?" I asked the tree, looking towards the creak. "Where is she?" There was another creak, further along the ceiling, then, where the ceiling met the far wall; Rogue and me following each sound. At the bottom of the wall, was a large basket. We crossed the room in two steps, and there, lying in the bottom, sleeping peacefully, was the stolen, baby Princess Elora.

CHAPTER 15

The Observatory

§§

"I don't think this is a normal sleep," Rogue was saying. "Surely she would have woken up by now?" Elora was cradled in my arms, still sleeping. We were back in our room behind the pale pink door.

"Not necessarily," I replied, rocking her gently. "But we need to get out of here before whoever took her sees she's gone. We need to get her back to the Queen."

"We don't know where the King and Queen went," Rogue pointed out, her head in her hands.

"Sure we do. They're with Ford and Evanna. They're the Guardian's family. People are bound to know where to find them!"

"Maybe so, but we can't go around announcing that we need to find them, can we? There are bound to be spies who would be very interested in hearing that."

The maples gave a deep rumble from the wall where all the brochures hung. "Seek and ye shall find!" I squeaked, going over to the wall. "Which one? They're all just tourist attractions!"

There was another loud creak, but not from the brochure wall. It came from the front door. "Rogue? Ranger?" a familiar voice called.

"Who is that?" I hissed, dropping down behind the bed to hide the baby.

Rogue shook her head, looking panicked. "The maples let them in," she quavered. "Surely that means-YOU!" she gasped, as the tall elven barman from the tavern came into the room. "Why are you here? How did you get in? And *how* do you know our names?" she demanded to know, her hands raised to strike.

The elf raised his hands defensively and stopped moving. "I mean you no harm," he said gently.

"How did you get in here," I heard Rogue repeat.

"My name is Jahra," he said. "The maples let me in."

"And why would they do that?"

"I assume for the same reason they let you into the dark green room," he answered tartly, crossing his arms.

"How do you know that?" Rogue was becoming more agitated. I could see her hands start to spark from my hiding place beside the bed. Princess Elora slept on.

"I am a member of the royal court. I was sent here as a spy to ferret out the leaders of the rebellion against the crown," he answered. "The maples care for all lives in

Valeria, so knowing I was trying to prevent bloodshed, they have helped me get information to Levindra by allowing me to examine certain private spaces," he went on, choosing each word delicately.

"They also told me your names… and where you were tonight. They tried to explain why, but the message was difficult to understand. The trees do not communicate as we do." I stood up from my hiding place and Jahra's mouth dropped open. "*Princess Elora?*" he exclaimed.

"SHHHH!" Rogue and I hissed together.

"Listen," I started. "We were in Levindra when the Capitol was put under siege. The Princess was kidnapped. The King and Queen escaped with the Guardian family, but we came looking for Elora. We need to get her back to her parents," I explained quickly. "Do you know where the Guardian's family lives?"

Jahra struggled to speak, opening and closing his mouth several times. "Ah. Y-yes, I do," he finally stuttered. "They are to the east; at the Observatory."

Armed with the map Ariannah had given us and the directions written on it by Jahra, who had promised to waylay the resident of the room behind the dark green door until we could get a decent head start, we set off towards the Observatory. We were wearing light cloaks provided by the maple trees; soft, warm moss on the inside, thick oak leaves on the outside, to protect us from the elements.

Elora was strapped to my chest in a woven wrap, also courtesy of the maples. She still hadn't stirred, but she was breathing steadily and her colour hadn't changed, so we assumed some sort of magic was keeping her in stasis. We hoped the Queen would know someone who could help.

"Based on the map, the Observatory is closer than the Capitol, but Ariannah said her house was a week away from Levindra on foot," I was telling Rogue as we flew. "We managed to get that far in a little over a night through the tunnels."

"So you think the tunnels are magic or that we can travel faster without realising?"

"I think the tunnels are definitely enchanted. Based on the same distance between Levindra and both Ariannah's and Farivian, the Observatory is about four days away."

"There's no way Elora can last that long without eating!" Rogue exclaimed. "We don't know when the last time she ate was as it is!"

"I know, but that is four days on foot. We're flying," I reminded her. "And I feel like we're moving a lot faster than we ever could walking, or even running. We need to make the most of the cool air by travelling through the night."

I'd come far in the day since I'd started flying. I couldn't stand not being able to feel my body against something solid, but necessity overpowered my fear. I certainly didn't revel in it the way Rogue seemed to. Her fear of heights had seemingly disappeared now she had wings. It was as though what made her feel like she had control and sedated her fear made me feel like I had none and exacerbated mine.

"Two sleepless nights in a row…" Rogue grumbled, interrupting my thoughts. "At least we have food this time." We fell silent and pushed on as fast as our previously unused wings would allow with our lack of practice, while the darkness deepened the further away from the city we became.

§

Dawn had broken. The last of the stars were quickly disappearing. We had covered far more ground than we could have hoped, but no matter how much bigger the Observatory was, it never seemed to get any closer.

Elora had begun to snuffle and whimper in her enchanted sleep. "I don't know how much longer she can stay like this," I said to Rogue, concerned.

"She'll be ok. We'll make it," she answered confidently, though I couldn't tell who exactly she was trying to convince.

"What if she's not?"

"She has to be."

Another three hours passed before we finally hit the ground and started running pell-mell through the short rough grass outside the Observatory, which rose fifty feet into the sky and whose circumference was that of the entire capital city of Levindra. It was built with intricately designed stone blocks that stacked together like the creator of Tetris had been the architect, and at the top, a long metal tube was sticking out of the roof, aimed at the sky.

Rogue had pulled out Ariannah's map and was reading Jahra's notes. "It says 'Pixie-Pivva. Crest-Evanna'," she panted as we reached the stone landing outside of the Observatory and rolled the map back up.

"Hello?" I called. "Can anyone hear us?" We walked around the base of the Observatory until we found a large steel door. "HELLO?"

A small window opened above the door and a bright purple head came out of it. "What's your business?" a voice drawled.

"We're here to see Pivva, the pixie?" Rogue yelled to the head. It groaned and pulled itself back through the window, before a grinding noise started, shaking the ground at our feet as the doors opened inward.

The purple head reappeared at the doors attached to a short, lithe body with long yellow wings. "Wait here please," they said, directing us to a bench just on the inside of the doors.

We sat down, Rogue offering me the water bag as I held baby Elora close, trying to comfort her through her whimpers. When the purple fairy returned, they were accompanied by an orange glow. When it dimmed, I could see the small, graceful figure of a pixie. "I'm sorry, do I know you?" Pivva inquired, a frown on her face.

"No!" Rogue said quickly. "We are your new students!"

Pivva continued to look suspicious. "I don't recall~"

"~Jahra sent us!" I interrupted, as the purple fairy also began to look perturbed. "Show her!" I hissed to Rogue, who pulled a small bag out of the satchel at her side and held it up to the pixie.

"Oh!" she squeaked, catching sight of the golden gleam of the royal crest inside. "Of course! I wasn't expecting you for weeks! I can't believe you were able to come so fast!" She fluttered around the purple fairy. "I'll take them from here, Rajan! Follow me!"

She turned and flew into the centre of the main foyer, which was open to the top of the Observatory, where a large skylight opened onto the heavens. Pivva began to fly up into the open space between the floors, leading us higher and higher.

We were almost at the top when she zipped to the left and stopped on the edge of a landing. "This way," she instructed briskly, nodding her head to the right hand corridor before she led us into a spacious, airy room that held nothing but a bed, a wooden desk, and another door.

The moment the door closed, she turned on us. "How could you be so reckless!" she snapped in outrage, her glow flashing angrily, inches from our faces.

"Excuse me?" Rogue exclaimed.

"Coming here, using Jahra's real name and pulling out the crest in public!" she spat. "What were you thinking?"

"We only did what Jahra told us to do!" Rogue snapped back. "We need to find the King and Queen. Now!"

"What?" Pivva paused, uncertain. "Jahra hasn't used his real name in almost a decade; not since the rebellion whispers started and he went into hiding. Now, we hear tell of attacks on the Capitol? What do you know about this?"

"We don't have time for your questions," I said bluntly, pulling aside my cloak and showing her the still sleeping Princess. "We know the royals are with Ford and Evanna. You need to take us to them immediately."

Pivva clapped her hand over her mouth, surprise, shock, anger, and fear all flitting across her face in a matter of seconds. "F-Ford and Evanna are on the top f-floor," she stammered quietly. "B-but there's no way the Queen could be here! The entire Observatory would know!"

"That's exactly why they travelled in secret. No one is to know where they are," I told her in a hushed whisper. "They're in danger."

"Danger?" Pivva repeated in a horrified gasp. "So it's true? The rebellion has reached the Capitol?" We both nodded grimly. "Oh no... we never thought it would come to this." Her face hardened. "Quickly, let's get you to Ford and Evanna's apartments."

The twenty four seconds it took to go from the meeting room, up twelve floors to the top landing, have Pivva knock on a large set of silver double doors, and have Evanna answer them with a muffled squeak, before pulling us across the threshold and slamming them shut, were some of the most agonising I'd ever felt.

"*Eleria come quickly!*" she cried out as she rushed us down the hallway to an open sitting area that was wall to wall grey stone. The sun shone through the clear ceiling high above us. "THEY'RE HERE!"

I heard the pounding of several doors opening and within moments the room held Evanna, Ford, Fillipe, six armed guards, Prince Fallon, King Evendon, and Queen Eleria. "What happened?" she asked. Her voice was harsh and demanding.

"We used the tunnels," Rogue told her. "After we hid the broken mirror, we figured out that if the rebels had used them to get in, then whoever took Elora had to as well."

I drew back my cloak and unwrapped the baby. The Queen gave a strangled gasp as I placed Elora in her arms. The tiny Princess chose that moment to yawn, stretch, and open her eyes, giving her mother a large, gummy grin. The Queen promptly burst into tears.

CHAPTER 16
Faeorah & The Glade

§§

"The symbol will allow you to reach Elva, through the magic protecting her. We can't risk assuming the Heart will recognise you," Queen Eleria instructed, holding a now well fed baby Elora to her chest, while she cooed softly and pulled at her long, dark hair.

We nodded and Rogue placed the crest around her neck, before her fairy self melted away, revealing a white, linen dress tied with a bright yellow thread. Her hair was black and curled, held back by a white headband, and her eyes flashed gold; her elven form.

"Wow," Evanna breathed. Rogue blushed.

After a final goodbye, we left the city. The further away we travelled, the less the magic worked. Soon, we were walking at a normal pace. By this time, the city of Faeorah was in sight. "We seriously need some of this magic wind at home," I said, breathing a sigh of relief, finally being able to relax ever so slightly after the terror involved of returning a kidnapped baby to her parents.

"It's the magic of the wind, Ranger; not magic wind," Rogue replied with a snort, shaking her head.

After a second full nights' sleep at a tavern called The Green Fairy, we planned our route to the southernmost area of Valeria on the map, where the Veritann River disappeared between the two mountain ranges; the Great Ranges where Ariannah lived, and a second mountain region known as the Snowy Rise.

"It will take about four days; three if we push ourselves," I told Rogue, examining Ariannah's map.

"Not familiar with that concept at all," she replied sarcastically.

"You know, between the Observatory, Ariannah's, the Marble Palace, and the room we found Elora in, almost every map has been different?" I queried.

"It makes sense given every one is hand made. No mass production here, remember?"

"Exactly!" I went on. "There's a symbol here on Arian-nah's map. Each person must have their own symbol when they draw their maps so they know it's theirs! I saw something similar on the map at The Lookout. If we can get a solid look at it, then we can identify who took Elora!" I finished trium-phantly.

"I'm not going back to Farivian," Rogue said flatly, her hands up. "Elora is safe with her parents. It took us long enough to get this far and we're too close to turn back now!"

"Maybe we don't have to."

At the reception desk of The Green Fairy was an array of bluebells. I ran my fingers along their petals, and a tinkling sound echoed through the lobby. Within seconds a bright purple light appeared in front of us.

"Good morning!" the pixie greeted us. "How was your stay?"

"Just perfect!" I responded gratuitously. "What would be the fastest way to get a message to Farivian?"

"Oh!" the purple light pulsed slightly. "That would be via tulip! The winds this time of year would see it arrive very quickly indeed!"

"Wonderful! I've never actually used one before. Can you help?"

"We don't keep any on the premises. You would have to head to the post gardens. Here are the directions!" the pixie replied, handing us a bark brochure.

"What are you sending?" Rogue asked as we walked around the hotel fountain.

"A message to Jahra," I answered. "We ask him about the symbol on the map and get him to see if there are any clues in the dark green room. If the map is still there, see if he can identify whose map it is. Get the information to the Queen," I stated orderly.

"And that will do what exactly?"

"It helps the Queen find the rebels that stole her baby!"

"Maybe, but that's still just one person," Rogue said. "Unless an effective solution is given to the public, the rebellion will still continue. They need to involve the other races more."

"One step at a time," I told her dismissively, as we crossed the threshold into the tulip gardens.

"Hello! Looking to send a message?" an elderly sprite with brown wings and a rough beard asked kindly.

"Yes please sir," I answered.

"Excellent! Where to?"

"Farivian? The Lookout Tavern."

"Okie dokie," he huffed as he bent down and plucked one of the larger white blossoms. He handed it to me. "Speak your name and recipient, then the message clearly into the tulip. It will carry your voice to the addressee and will only open for them. Understand?"

"Yes sir! Thank you!" I grinned, cupping the bloom gently in my hands. "What if the recipient isn't where we think he is?"

"Oh, worry not about that, dear," he said reassuringly. "The tulip will find him."

Rogue paid the tulip man and we left the gardens. "What now?" she asked.

"We send the message and keep heading for the Ranges. His response should find us," I answered. I spoke into the tulip and when I was finished, the petals closed tightly. As we watched, it drifted into the sky and floated away on the breeze.

As I watched it, my mind wandered. I thought about everything that had happened so far. It humbled me to know that the Heart of Ventura was our responsibility to reunite, but that didn't make the idea any less terrifying to consider.

I thought about our family; about our parents and where they were. It worried me the most because I didn't know what would happen to them if they went back to the castle before we did. I thought about Reina and Rowan, wondering how much they hated us right now because we'd finally removed them from the castle.

Then I wondered if we would even manage to survive long enough to convince the Guardian to give us the Heart of Valeria and get home at all.

"Come on, we can't wait any longer," Rogue urged, breaking me from my trance. We grew our wings and headed for Faeorah's southern gates, in the opposite direction to the tulip's destination.

§

We'd been travelling for two days when we reached the lush, green jungle that surrounded the foothills. The mountains of the Snowy Rise were looming above us. They were twice, if not three times as high as the Great Ranges. The snow of the higher altitudes came almost halfway down the steep slopes.

"Do we go through it, or around?" I asked Rogue.

She looked through the trees, considering both options. "Around would be easier, but straight through would cut at least a day off the travel time."

"We could fly over?"

"I don't like the sound of that. We don't know how long these trees go on for and the canopy is so thick you can't see through it. If we got tired and needed to land, there'd be no way of knowing if we could without getting attacked by something."

"And there's no way of knowing if we'd be attacked just by flying over to begin with," I agreed. Rogue nodded. "Through?"

"Through. It'll be nice to get out of the heat." We stepped into the darkness of the thick forest and instantly, the high mid-morning heat disappeared.

There was no real path through the trees, so we plotted our direction and weaved between them, keeping as true to our course as possible. If we needed to confirm we hadn't turned off course, then we could always fly above the canopy to check, but we wanted to avoid it if we could, unsure of what creatures called the treetops home. Over the initial hours of our trek, we had already heard a loud screech from the sky above us, an odd clicking noise from the trees, and a deep growl from off in the distance that had us fleeing as fast as our feet and wings could carry us. We'd only stopped because we could no longer take a breath, but once we did, the source of the growling, whatever it had been, had stopped.

Outside of those eerie events, the forest was calm and quiet; almost peaceful if it weren't for the constant fear of attack. The grass was soft under our feet and the air was cool and moist. The cities had been beautiful, but with no people to care for and the ability to grow as they saw fit, the trees seemed so much more radiant.

"I didn't realise there were this many shades of green," I thought out loud as we entered a glade. There was a large, round pool, fed by a small waterfall. "Wow!" There were all kinds of wildflowers surrounding the edge of the glade, giving off a heavenly scent. The brightness of the colours was a stark and welcome contrast to the similar green hues of the rest of the forest. As I gazed at the pool, my thirst hit me like a train. I would have started drooling if I hadn't been so dehydrated. Our waterskins had been drained the previous day.

"Well, this looks like a well placed trap," Rogue announced bluntly.

"What?" I exclaimed. "It's a pond in a forest. They happen. Geez, lighten up."

"Oh, so you don't think it's suspicious that there's no village, town, or city around here?" she shot back sceptically.

"All this natural beauty, strong, sturdy trees, water sources, gorgeous scenery of the mountains, and everyone in Valeria went 'no thanks'?"

"Rogue, you're thinking too far into it," I sighed. "It's just a forest. There are plenty of places for the people of Valeria to live. It's not like home, where every piece of land must be used by people. They respect nature here. Of course, there's going to be places left untouched!"

Rogue did not seem convinced. "We need to be careful. We don't know where we are, what's around, or what dangers exist that we're just not familiar with because we've been here a week!" she lectured, frustrated. "For all we know there's a tripwire and cannibals will get us, or the water is poisoned, or this is the home of whatever was growling earlier and we're just standing here offering ourselves up as an easy lunch!"

"What would you suggest?" I asked in an attempt to placate her.

She scanned the glade, then pointed to a large oak to our right. "Climb and wait. If there's something here, it won't stick around forever; it'll either make itself known or leave."

"And how long do you propose we do that?"

She paused, considering the question. "A few hours, I guess?"

"*Hours?* Are you kidding?" I was so thirsty.

"Shh!" Rogue hissed. "You don't know what's listening!"

"PLANTS, ROGUE! PLANTS ARE LISTENING!" I exploded. "We can't afford to waste hours! We need to find Elva and get home!"

I started stomping across the glade, dodging Rogue's grip as I pulled the water skin from my satchel to refill it. "Ranger! We can't be rash! WAIT!" she yelled, chasing after me. I dodged her again and dunked the water skin into the clear pool.

"See?" I snapped smugly. "Cool; clear; perfectly healthy."

I was right. The water was perfectly fine; clean and crisp and wonderfully refreshing. Unfortunately, Rogue was also right; something was watching us. As we were arguing, we hadn't noticed the large purple flower on the edge of the glade had fully opened, revealing the jagged jaws of an enormous venus fly trap. I was proven right for a second time; the plants really had been listening, as it lunged forward and trapped Rogue in its jaws.

CHAPTER 17

Vincit Omnia Veritas

§§

"NO!" I screamed as the monstrous venus started dragging her back to its place at the edge of the glade. As I lunged forward in an attempt to grab her exposed legs, it snapped a second time and they disappeared too. "ROGUE!"

I could hear her muffled screaming from deep within the plant's gullet. I was starting to lose my ability to form a coherent thought as the panic took over. "Come on, *think!*" I told myself, huffing as I struggled to breathe properly. I remembered the mirror Rogue and I destroyed in the Marble Palace. Could I pull it off again? Alone?

"Ok," I whispered to myself. I held my hands out to the plant and concentrated. It had stilled, but I could still hear Rogue thrashing and crying out from inside. I didn't have a lot of time. "Come on; please," I begged. Nothing happened.

I dropped my hands helplessly and instead, threw myself at the beast, clawing at it with my bare hands. "Ranger!" I heard Rogue call out to me. I froze as I felt my hands start to tingle and heat up.

"ROGUE!" I yelled back. "HOLD ON!" I pushed more of the energy into my hands and they grew hotter. The venus started thrashing about, clearly in pain, but I wasn't letting go.

Finally, there was a poisonous hiss and a growling croak from deep within the plant as my hands caught fire and the venus fly trap went up in flames. I threw my hands into the blaze and as soon as I felt Rogue's body, I pulled with all my strength. With a loud, squelching noise that could be heard over the crackling of the flames, Rogue was dislodged and came flying out of the fiery belly of the beast, the both of us hitting the grass of the glade; gasping for air.

As soon as I caught my breath, I rolled over and got to my feet, stumbling towards the pool. I thrust my hands into the water, tapping into the same energy I'd used to create the fire, and sent the water spiralling from its rocky bed to the burning venus fly trap, dousing the flames before it could spread to the rest of the forest.

When I had finished, I dropped back down next to Rogue and placed my hand on her arm. "Are you ok?" I panted. She raised her finger in a signal to give her a minute. "Yeah, yeah, I know… You told me so."

§

Despite the delay at the glade, the shortcut through the forest eventually paid off. We reached the end of the trees as the last rays of the sun were disappearing behind the Great Ranges.

"Do you think you can eat?" I asked Rogue, after lighting a fire and setting up our bedrolls.

"After almost being eaten myself, I don't think it's something I ever want to do again," she answered, eyes closed.

"I'm sorry I didn't listen to you," I said softly.

"I know."

"I don't know what I'd do if I ever lost you." In that moment, I was so overwhelmed with the thought that I started crying and couldn't stop. "I almost got you killed!" I sobbed.

"It'll take a lot more than an overgrown weed to take me down," she answered, slapping my knee half-heartedly.

"I am a lot more than an overgrown weed. I was rash and you were right; we don't know where we are or what's around and I can't keep acting like this is home. It's not."

"You're learning. That's the best we can hope for." We climbed into our bedrolls, but if Rogue's night was anything like mine, neither of us slept.

§

The next morning we'd packed away our gear and were on our way before the sun had fully risen. We walked side by side, completely silent. I couldn't imagine what was going through Rogue's mind, but the air was tense, like a rubber band ready to snap.

I physically couldn't speak. It was common for me. I had found myself in this position many times before. I'd do something without thinking and someone would get hurt. Usually, it was feelings and I felt horrible every time, desperately wishing I could think faster than I could act, so things like that would stop happening. This time was different. This time it very easily could have cost my sister her life.

I kept replaying the scene of what happened in my head. Me; filling up my waterskin, Rogue; following me, the venus fly trap coming out of nowhere, its gaping maw closing over her… I'd panicked. Even when it mattered, I'd frozen. Even when it meant her life, I couldn't respond properly.

I was so fully trapped within my own mind that I didn't even notice when Rogue started talking to me, or that from the moment we hit the foothills, there had been a sudden shift in the winds.

"What was that?" Rogue was calling to me. "RANGER!" Before I could answer, a huge shadow covered us and there was a loud screech from high above our heads, the same one we had heard from above the canopy the day before. We spun around and found a huge, feathered creature plunging towards us, talons outstretched. It had a giant blue plume coming out of its head and its feathers gave off the look of scaled armour. Rogue let loose an ear-splitting scream, frozen to the spot. I dove toward her, knocking her out of the way. The creature turned and circled back around, preparing for another assault.

"GET TO THE CLIFFS!" I roared to her. "FIND A CAVE!" We flew towards the vast lilac coloured mountains, ducking and weaving in an attempt to dodge the beast, its monstrous shadow keeping pace with us with no apparent difficulty. There was another screech. We flew faster. My lungs were aching and I felt like my heart was on the verge of giving out. We were twenty feet from the nearest cliff face… fifteen feet… ten feet.

At five feet there was another piercing screech, but this was one of pain. We spun around and found the bird like beast flying in the opposite direction, an arrow in its side, still screeching. Out of a crevice among the rock on the mountains of the Rise, came a large, yellow fairy with bright blonde curly hair. "Are you alright?" she called, helping us to our feet. "You should have informed us of your arrival! We would have sent an escort!"

"We didn't know that's what we had to do!" Rogue tried to explain, attempting to straighten out her wing.

"Well, what are you doing in these parts? Not a common place for exploring; the Whispers isn't!"

"The Whispers?" Rogue repeated.

"We were sent by the Queen," I said.

"The Queen?" she frowned, her mouth slightly agape. "You had better come inside, hadn't you?"

She escorted us through the crevice and into a large brightly lit cave that had been hollowed out of the mountain. In the centre of the cave grew a towering willow tree, just like the one that covered the entrance to the Farivian escape tunnel. "How does it grow here?" Rogue gasped in amazement.

"Magic," an elven man with knee length blood red dreadlocks replied, walking over to us holding a bow, the quiver hanging across his back.

"You shot the bird?" I breathed, my heart still racing. "You saved us?"

The elf frowned and nodded, "It was a Vertracian."

"Vertracian… right," I replied as I stared up at the tree.

"You're… not from around here, are you?" he asked, confused. He surveyed us suspiciously, clearly unsure how to proceed. "You said the Queen sent you here? But you weren't warned of the Vertracian?"

"Not here exactly; further south," I corrected, my voice wavering slightly. "I don't think she expected us to be this far east. We were meant to follow the river, but… got lost."

If anything, he became more suspicious. "There is nothing further south from here," he said quietly, looking us up and down. He took a slow deliberate step forward and picked up the royal crest from around Rogue's neck. His body seemed to pause for a split second before he let it drop.

"We are Vincit Omnia Veritas, the protectors of this pass… and all within it," he said deliberately, taking a step closer so he was less than a foot away. "Many have come here trying to hide their true intentions, but they are always made clear in the end. Honesty conquers all things. Vincit Omnia Veritas!"

"VINCIT OMNIA VERITAS!" the other soldiers chanted back.

"We won't lie to you," Rogue told him evenly. "But we can't tell you why we're here, either."

He raised an eyebrow and surveyed her curiously, before standing aside and directing her to the tree. "Place the crest in the hollow," he instructed softly, aware of some protocol that we, evidently, were not.

Rogue crept forward slowly, flew up to the nook high above her head. She gently removed the royal crest from around her neck and pressed it into the hollow. There was a bright pink flash from within and the crest disappeared, leaving in its place, a pale green river stone in the shape of a heart. It hovered in front of her eyes, before dropping into her hand. She squeezed it tightly. "We'll take care of it, we promise," she told the elf.

He led us away from the tree and escorted us to the edge of the Vertracian's territory. "Are you sure you know what you're doing?" he asked, hesitant to leave us.

"No," I answered plainly. "But we still have to go." He gave a final concerned look, before nodding slowly and heading back along the mountain cliffs.

The mountain ranges were separated by the flowing Veritann River and its adjacent road that led to a waterfall. It flowed down the south eastern cliff face of the snowy tops above. When the sun began to go down, we set up camp.

The wind had died down and the fire was alight. Rogue was playing with her left wing. She preferred to travel flying. "How is it that we ended up here?" she said suddenly, lying down on her unrolled feather mattress. We'd each been given one by Fillipe, an avid camper, as well as a letter he had secretly asked us to give his sister. Evanna had also seen to it that we were given provisions and a letter for Elva from her parents. The letter Fillipe had given us was hidden with it.

"We were living our lives; took a wrong turn somewhere. When we tried to get back, we tripped and went too far," I answered with a sigh.

"And now we're responsible for the welfare of seven worlds worth of people."

"Eight if you count ours."

Rogue groaned in response.

CHAPTER 18

Elva

§§

The waterfall was thundering down in front of us. Its spray had already drenched us through and our skin was chilled. We faced the yawning cave mouth at the top. We could feel the Heart calling out to us. It was close and we somehow knew that the Guardian felt that we were coming.

"IT'S TOO EASY!" I yelled to Rogue over the din.

"WHAT DO YOU MEAN? YOU CALL GETTING TO *THAT* EASY?"

"NO! I MEAN THAT YOU CAN SEE IT ALL TOO EASY! THE GUARDIAN'S SANCTUARY WOULD BE PRIVATE! A PLACE YOU CAN'T SEE!"

"WHERE?" she yelled to me. I pointed to the waterfall. "YOU THINK THERE'S A CAVE BEHIND THE WATERFALL?"

"THERE'S ONLY ONE WAY TO FIND OUT!" I rose into the air until I was opposite the centre of the waterfall. Then, before I could think too long about it and change my mind, I took a deep breath and shot forward, forcing myself through the water as it pounded down on me.

The water didn't let up. I started to panic. Just when I was nearing the point of no return, where I would attempt to open my mouth for air and find only water, I fell through the other side.

I let myself fall forward to the ground as I gulped in lungful after lungful of damp, freezing air.

When I finally managed to get my bearings, I stood up and looked around, but this side of the waterfall was a veil of darkness. As my eyes adjusted to the dark and the water drained from my ears, I noticed that there was a gentle pink glow coming from the end of the vast cavern… and an ominous screaming coming from behind me. Rogue shot out of the waterfall, pulling herself up before she crashed into the ground. "Don't *do* that! We *just had* this conversation!"

"That was before the same rash behaviour that almost got you killed saved you from the Vertracian… and found the Guardian's hideout," I puffed, still catching my breath, as I continued to stare at the glow.

Rogue followed my gaze. "Do we follow it?"

"Too late to turn back now." We started for the back of the cavern, dodging around stalactites and stalagmites, flying over puddles of standing water.

We'd only made it a third of the way across when the waterfall exploded and a dozen or so soldiers landed neatly on the rock floor, barely hitting the ground before they leapt up and started sprinting towards us.

"WE WERE FOLLOWED! FLY!" I shrieked, taking off into the air, which was just as difficult as running due to all the hulking piles of stone throughout the cavern.

"Who are they?" Rogue yelled.

"Rebels! Vincit Omnia Veritas! They knew where we were going all along! They used us to find Elva! We have to get to her first! This will be all our fault if something happens to her!"

Rogue looked pale and terrified as we struggled to lose our pursuers, but they were gaining on us every second. "Stop!" she finally cried, freezing in mid air.

"Are you kidding?" I screeched. "WE CAN'T STOP!"

"We have to," she said, shaking her head. "We'll never be able to outpace them, flying or not."

"So what, we just die and let the same happen to Elva?" I snapped angrily.

She turned to me, eerily calm. "No," she whispered. She looked to her hands, holding them out in front of her. They began to glow; a deep, pulsating, golden glow. "We protect her."

I looked into her eyes; committed, determined, resolute. She was right. Running would help nobody. Now was the time; time to prove who we were and what we could do; to protect the legacy Romira built.

I nodded, and let my wings slip away as I took my elven form, hitting the ground and rolling into a crouch as I pulled a bow from my shoulder and an arrow from the newly appeared quiver on my back.

"Please, please, please, please, please," I whispered with my eyes closed before I snapped them open and loosed the first arrow. It arched through the air and struck the nearest fairy soldier in the shoulder. "YES!"

There was a roar from one of the other soldiers, a short, stocky, tank of a sprite, with an orange beard that reached his feet. He came flying toward me at full speed and in fear, I froze. He was barely a foot away when a shot of golden light hit him in the side and knocked him off course, sending him crashing into one of the stalactites. Rogue.

And so the onslaught continued. No matter how many enemies we struck down, more seemed to take their place. We couldn't tell if there were more coming through the waterfall, or if the ones we were hitting were just not staying down.

At one point during the battle, my bow was wrestled from my grip by a short, athletic fairy, who managed to dodge every shot I took at her, before robbing me of my weapon. As I stared at the smug look on her face, desperate for another weapon, my own hands began to glow, a deep acid green aura surrounding me. Instead of shooting it at the smirking fairy, I willed all of my power into my right hand, drew back, and punched her square in the face, sending her flying backward and into a puddle of water with a splash.

"Ranger!" I heard Rogue cry. I found her in the crowd, knocking away opponent after opponent. When she caught my eye, she pointed. I followed her finger and my jaw dropped. It was a tulip.

I'd paused for too long. I was struck in the side by a dagger wielded by a sprite with blood red wings and white blonde braids. In my panic, I wrenched out the dagger and drove it into her shoulder blade before I pressed my hand down over the wound. She screamed and reeled backward, clearing the path ahead of me.

I started to draw from the energy building at my core, pushing it further into my remaining hand. As I prepared to unleash it, everything suddenly went quiet. The noise of the battle became a low hum like I was wearing earplugs, and everyone appeared to be moving in slow motion.

I looked around the cavern, and spotted Rogue halfway across it, standing on the ground. I waved to get her attention. Her face flooded with relief when she saw me. I pointed to my ear and held up my arms questioningly. She covered her ears and shook her head, confusion on her face.

Hello Rogue and Ranger

A voice that was not my own, drifted into my head. Rogue's eyes widened. She pointed at her ear. I nodded back, confirming that I could hear it too. The glowing at the end of the cavern grew tenfold. We turned to the light, shielding our eyes.

Are you… the Heart of Romira? I asked the voice, project-
ing my thoughts.

Once. Now, I am known as the Heart of Valeria.

Instead of pounding, as I had expected it to, my heart felt
like it had stopped altogether. My breath came in short, sharp
gasps and I felt like my vision was flickering. I forced myself
to think calmly.

*Raven split you into seven pieces to save the Romira's
worlds from Raphael… your son. We have come to reunite
them.*

*My son? Yes… I remember. Raven committed a great crime
by doing what she did.*

*Surely you believe seven hearts protecting the Venturan
Worlds is better than one Heart destroying them, and she sent
us to fix it; to make you whole again.*

There was a calculating pause. *I see that you speak the
truth. The Guardian knows of you, but she is wary.*

Where is she?

I am here already. The new voice was lighter but heavy
with exhaustion.

Are you Elva?

*Once. Now, I am the Guardian. Who are you? Why have
you brought a battle to my doorstep?*

*My name is Ranger. This is my sister; Rogue. The soldiers
followed us from Vincit Omnia Veritas. They're trying to
overtake the Capitol and dethrone the Queen.*

Rogue and Ranger? The light flickered, and through it, we could see a humanoid shape. *That cannot be possible. Vincit Omnia Veritas serves the Queen. They guard the entrance to my home. They act as my final line of defence.*

They must have been corrupted somehow. They used us to find you. Rogue told her.

Is the Queen safe?

We don't know. They were safe when we left her, the King and their children with your parents and brother at the Observatory. We have letters from them for you.

The light flickered again at the mention of her parents. *Do you know your legend here, Rogue and Ranger?* Her voice came in powerful waves.

We know Raven told your world that we would come for the Heart. Will you give it to us?

She didn't answer immediately. *No. I have work to do with it, especially if what you say about the uprising in the Capitol, and Vincit Omnia Veritas being overrun, is correct.*

You don't believe us?

You are saying what you believe to be true, yes. That doesn't mean you are right. We shall discuss this once I am finished.

She fell silent and the pulsing pink glow began to grow, until it filled the entire cavern, surrounding each of the incoming soldiers. When the light died down, each and every one of them had disappeared without a trace.

Rogue and I looked around quickly, confirming the danger was over, before turning back to Elva. Ever so slowly, the glow withdrew into her body, illuminating her skin, and the light dulled to a throbbing pulse at her throat, which allowed us to see her more distinctly.

She was shorter than me and built like an athlete. Her blonde ringlets were held back with a laurel band, before falling about her round face and down over her shoulders. Her eyes were small and round, glowing a bright blue from within. Her skin was pale and freckly. She wore a light purple cloak buttoned at the waist with long sleeves and a hood. Her green shirt and tights could be seen underneath, and her brown boots came up to her knees. Large pink wings with red membranes spider webbing across them sprouted out of her shoulder blades and towered above us at almost twice her height. The only evidence of her elven heritage was her sharp, pointed ears.

The glow continued to retreat into her body like she was sucking it out of the very air; drawing it back to where it came from. As the light finally dissipated, she lowered herself to the ground and held her head high as she walked steadily through to cavern, to where Rogue and I were waiting, awestruck.

I still held my hand to my side, putting pressure on the wound. She held out her hand and touched her fingertips to my forehead. Instantly, the pain disappeared.

"Wow!" I gasped, as I gulped in my first full lungful of air since I was hit. "Thank you!"

Elva said nothing. She simply turned her hand over, so her palm faced upward expectantly. "The letters. The letters!" Rogue whispered quickly, grabbing them from my satchel. She handed them to Elva, who opened them delicately and began reading. When she finished, she gave a great sigh, folded up the letters, and placed them gently in a pocket within the folds of her cloak.

"So Vincit Omnia Veritas has been infiltrated?" she asked calmly as if a horde of assassins were something she dealt with on a daily basis.

"We think so. We don't know who they're taking orders from," I answered.

"Wait!" Rogue gasped. "The tulip! Where is it?"

We rapidly scanned the cave. "There!" I yelped, leaping across the cavern floor and collecting the delicate white flower from one of the pools.

"Why is this tulip important?" Elva asked.

"It might tell us who kidnapped the Princess," Rogue answered. "We sent it to Jahra in Farivian, where we found her." Elva's eyes narrowed. She nodded and went silent.

I held up the tulip and stroked the petals to remove the water. At my touch, the petals opened and Jahra's voice was projected out of the centre, crisp and clear.

Rogue and Ranger, I am pleased to hear of the return of the baby Princess. I have searched the dark green room, which, oddly, remains intact. It appears as though it were abandoned as nothing has been removed.

I examined the map in question, and you are correct, there is a sigil in the upper corner. This isn't something you usually see on map works. Marking personal maps is not a common practice. I've included a drawing with the tulip, for your reference.

I will continue investigations to locate the owner of these maps and inform you should I find anything.

Good luck.

I pulled open the tulip and on the back of one of the petals was a symbol lightly drawn in green glossy ink. "Oh no," I breathed.

"You recognise this symbol?" Elva asked.

"Yes," Rogue huffed, pulling our map from my satchel and unrolling it, exposing the exact symbol in the upper right corner.

"Ariannah," I whispered.

"Ariannah," Rogue nodded darkly.

Elva looked deeply disturbed. "It would appear that we're not finished yet," she declared, waving a glowing hand through the air. A mirror appeared, with a silver frame made of thorny vines. "Shall we?" she asked in a tired voice, stepping through the mirror.

CHAPTER 19

Back In The Capitol

§§

Levindra had been thrown into chaos. Elves, fairies, sprites and pixies alike were all fleeing for their lives, as explosions erupted all around us. From the grounds of the Marble Palace, we could see thorny vines forcing themselves out of the ground to form a menacing wall. Throughout the city, healers were mending wounds and tending to dozens of ancient, uprooted trees.

"How do we get~? OW!" Rogue asked, resting her hands on the vine wall and pricking herself on a thorn. "Climbing won't work. Flying?"

"We can always try, but if I know Ariannah, she will have thought of that," Elva answered, methodically considering every inch of the wall in front of us.

"You know Ariannah?" I asked, surprised. "How?"

"Not directly, but most in the royal inner circle know of her, at least. Stand back." We complied, as the Guardian necklace began to glow. The light washed over Elva and crashed against the vined wall in wave after wave of force, until something within gave way, and a hole was blown through to the other side.

Almost as immediately as it appeared, the vines from the untouched sections of the walls whipped out and started spider webbing across the gaping hole in the Marble Palace's defences. "GO GO GO!" I screamed, sprinting for the steadily closing gap, Rogue and Elva on my heels.

We dove through the hole and landed roughly on the other side. The vines started lashing out at us, clawing at our feet and ankles in an attempt to drag us back through the wall. Just as we managed to get to our feet, I felt thorns pierce the flesh of my calves and I lost my balance, crashing flat on my face. I tried to cry out in pain, but nothing came out. In desperation, I clawed at the vines, but to no avail.

I was dragged backward with increasing ferocity and speed. I spun over so I was being dragged on my back instead, and I saw how close I was to being engulfed by the wall. As more vines reached out and the very real terror at the thought of being mummified overcame me, a bright piercing light cut through the vines and my body came to a skidding halt.

"Are you ok?" Rogue asked me, sliding across the last few feet of grass to my side and cupping my face in her hands. I still couldn't speak, so I just nodded, looking down at the mangled mess of blood my legs had become.

"Take a deep breath," Elva instructed me. She waited until I had fully breathed in, before placing a hand on either leg. I released the breath as a strangled cry, then the pain was gone. The blood, however, remained.

"Are you ok?" Rogue repeated, pale as a sheet.

"I'll be fine," I answered, my breath coming in short puffs. "Given recent events, I have a feeling that won't be the worst thing we face today."

"INDEED NOT" a deep sonorous voice boomed across the palace grounds.

Ariannah stood by the open palace doors, an acid green aura covering her body, her hair floating around her eerily. We gazed up at her from the bottom of the stairs.

"Do not interfere," she warned, her hands raised. "The royals have brought this upon themselves."

"Even you can't stand against the power of the Heart, Ariannah," Elva warned, starting up the stairs. "Valeria's issues may be rooted in the monarchy, but a war will not resolve it!"

"Oh, I'm not here to dismantle the monarchy," Ariannah announced; a grim smile on her lips. "I'm here to take it. For too long the royal family used my power to benefit themselves, all the while dismissing and devaluing my existence and that of those like me, who don't fall into their consideration of normal. Welcome to the consequences of their actions."

She closed her fists in a snapping motion and further explosions were heard in the distance. "ARIANNAH STOP!

THERE ARE *CHILDREN* OUT THERE!" Rogue screamed desperately over the noise as I held my hands over my ears.

Ariannah dropped her hands and met her eyes. They were cold; empty. "So?"

"*How can you be so heartless?*" I spat angrily, and took to the stairs, jumping two at a time. She regarded me for a moment before she flung out her arm and all three of us were launched back across the grass. When we got back to our feet, Ariannah was disappearing through the main doors, and with a flick of her wrist, they slammed shut.

"We have to get to her," Rogue fretted. "She'll destroy the whole city if we don't."

Elva shook her head in distress. She looked near tears. "I don't understand. How is she overpowering the magic of the Heart? Nothing ever has before!"

"It'll be ok," I promised her. "You're not alone."

She looked up at me and nodded shakily. "We split up. Find her. Alert the others when we do."

Rogue and I nodded in agreement and we all took off in different directions. Once at the top of the stairs, I made for the doors, but I wasn't able to get them open. I took a step back and evaluated my choices. I could circle the palace walkways looking for another entrance… or I could take my chances with one of the balconies and hope that a door was unlocked and that Ariannah didn't see me coming.

I made the call to risk it. There was a balcony roughly thirty metres above me, and if I flew fast enough, I could be there in less than ten seconds. After a final double glance along the walkways on either side of me, I opened my wings and shot upwards as fast as I could. When I landed on the balcony, I immediately dropped to the floor, my heart pounding, waiting for the inevitable attack.

When none came, I glanced through the doorway and saw nothing blocking my entry but a sheer curtain. On the other side was a lavish suite with the biggest four poster bed I'd ever seen, dressed in rich blue linens.

"Ok, get to the hallway. Keep your ears open and stay out of sight," I whispered softly to myself. An idea suddenly came to me that would help me do just that. I closed my eyes and concentrated. "Come on… come on, come on, come on," I groaned. I started to feel the tingle in my fingertips. "Yes!"

Everything around me grew significantly larger, as I shrunk down into my pixie form. I didn't have the chance to investigate it though. As soon as I figured out how to use the wings, which worked quite differently from the fairy wings I was used to, I did a quick check of the hallway and started searching the palace for Ariannah.

The top floors were seemingly empty of all citizens, but multiple times I had to hide behind suits of armour or a tapestry to avoid the countless guards that were patrolling the halls. As I neared the ground floor, I started hearing a methodical thudding coming from the back of the palace. Sure enough, as I followed the sound, I found it was leading me to the throne room.

"Bring her in!" Ariannah's voice demanded from inside. I watched from the hallway entrance as two guards dragged a limp, unconscious Rogue through the doors.

My heart was racing. I couldn't believe I'd let this happen. We were never apart, and the one time before now that we had been, it was a long planning process that took months of preparation. This time, we'd just... left. In the heat of the moment we'd taken off in different directions without a moment's hesitation and now she'd been captured.

My mind was running twenty different scenarios and not a single one was going to work if I rushed in. After what had happened with the venus fly trap, I couldn't put her at risk again. Who knew that the potential death of a loved one was a natural remedy to ADHD?

I examined the crowd and saw multiple pixies, all as small glowing balls of light. "Blue," I whispered. "Plenty of blue out there. I should blend right in." I focused on the blue colours I could see and hoped that no one would realise one more blue pixie had joined the throng outside the throne room.

When I was sure I looked right, I joined the group and made for Rogue as quickly as I dared, holding my breath the whole way. Just as she was pulled across the threshold and into the throne room beyond, I leapt forward, channelling as much energy from my core as I could and pushing it into my hands. When I unleashed it, both guards went flying through the doors and halfway across the foyer. Before the remaining rebel soldiers could react, I sent another wave at the doors and they slammed shut.

"Welcome, girls," Ariannah's voice taunted sweetly. "How kind of you to join us, Ranger. I'm so glad we didn't have to hunt you down like we did your sister… or dear Elva."

I changed back into my elven form and dropped to Rogue's side. As soon as I felt a pulse and heard her groan, I looked up and found Ariannah sitting delicately on the throne; Elva tied up and hanging from the chandelier above her, a trickle of blood dripping down her arm. "You led us here on purpose. You wanted us to find Elva and lead her straight to you."

"And by so doing, deliver the three biggest threats to my control of Valeria!" she responded, smiling broadly. "Thank you for your assistance. I couldn't have done it without you."

"We won't let you do this," Rogue groaned. I spun to face her. She slowly got to her feet and wiped her bloody nose with the back of her arm.

"I don't see how you propose to stop me," Ariannah responded condescendingly. "Royce or not, you have no more power here than a standard citizen!" she jeered.

"We came to make sure Valeria is protected, and one way or another, that's exactly what we'll do," I answered, mirroring her arrogant tone.

She raised an eyebrow as I took Rogue's hand. I glanced up at Elva. She looked pale. Her lips had lost all colour. We didn't have a lot of time. "Can you do this?" I asked Rogue, eyes locked on Ariannah, who had stood from the throne.

"I'll be fine," Rogue answered, still breathing heavily. "Ready?"

"Ready." I reached into the hard knot nestled in the pit of my stomach and pulled everything I had out of it. Electricity shot through my body and electrified me from my toes up, sparks crackling between the strands of my hair as it flew up around me.

A secondary wave zapped through me as Rogue's power intermingled with mine. It made my eyes water, but I could still see Ariannah's smug visage turn to outrage at the turn of events.

As the power grew, Ariannah drew back her sleeves and started chanting. I couldn't hear it over the sound of the pounding in my ears. We just had to hope we finished before she could.

We didn't make it. The moment she stopped chanting, she balled her fists and started hurling balls of orange energy at us. I wasn't even able to flinch; we were locked in place.

It turned out it didn't matter.

The ball of energy hit us full force and glanced right off. It struck a pillar off to our left and some of the stone started to crumble away. This just caused Ariannah to double her efforts, hurling ball after ball at us, desperate to break through. Each one glanced off our electric shield, hitting the walls around us. Above our heads, larger pieces of marble started to fall.

"Now?" I asked Rogue.

"Now!" she called back, and we raised our hands, aiming them right at Elva.

Ariannah threw her arm up to shield herself but paused when there was no impact. The electrical force arched across the room and struck Elva. Her body began to absorb it. Ariannah's anger intensified as she redoubled her efforts in the assault. Elva began to glow.

"Keep going!" Rogue yelled. I forced everything I had out my palms and into Elva. She began to shudder, until the rope that bound her snapped and she disappeared within the blinding white light that surrounded her, a chunk of the roof coming down with the chandelier she had been suspended from.

When Elva reappeared, she was surrounded by her pink glow once again. Her skin was no longer ashy and sunken, and her eyes glowed brighter than the sun. Ariannah looked mutinous. "THE HEART WON'T PROTECT YOU, ELVA!" she roared.

Despite the noise of marble slabs dropping from the ceiling all around us, and how calmly Elva spoke, her voice still came out clear and vibrant. "I don't need it to." She clapped her hands together, and when she opened them slightly, a white ball of light started growing between them, fed by the energy Rogue and I were still pouring into her.

"You can still walk away, Ariannah!" I called to her. "It doesn't have to end like this!"

"I DIDN'T COME THIS FAR TO THROW IT ALL AWAY!" she screamed, raising her hands high above her head.

Elva struck first. She pushed her hand forward and shot the white, glowing ball of energy directly at Ariannah, where it hit her directly in the chest. She appeared to choke and gasp, before dropping to the floor. As soon as she hit the ground, so did Rogue, breaking the connection between the three of us.

"We have to get out! The palace is coming down!" I yelled over the horrendous grating sound that was coming from all around us.

"Take Rogue and go!" Elva demanded, and she ran to Ariannah's fallen body.

"WHAT ARE YOU DOING?"

"I'll be right behind you just *go!*"

As a giant crack appeared under my feet, I pulled Rogue onto my shoulders and fled the throne room.

CHAPTER 20

The Idea

§§

The Marble Palace was in ruins. The people were terrified. Ariannah's body lay on the grass a short way away. Just like the soldiers who had followed us into the Guardian's lair, the entire horde of rebels who had overrun Levindra had vanished. Rogue had been healed and was sitting beside me on a chunk of marble sticking out of the ground.

I was shaking my head. "How do we fix this?" I asked helplessly, crouching to the ground.

"The damage to the palace and city is all physical," Elva said from what used to be the top of the stairs leading into the palace foyer. "The trees are healing as we speak. This is easy; the damage to Valeria, however… The world has lost its faith in the structure with which they live their lives. That is a far greater issue that must be rectified if Valeria is to survive, or it will only create more Ariannahs. For whatever reason, she was immune to the power of the Heart. Hopefully, she is a one of a kind case, but I don't want to have to find out. For now…" She held her hands out to her sides, before clapping them together at her chest, eyes closed. A glow started from the golden necklace at her throat and continued building until it had illuminated the entirety of the palace grounds, including us. "Don't move."

Rogue and I complied, firmly planting our feet as we watched Elva's magic. The shattered remnants of marble all came together into huge slabs, that lifted into the sky and landed back on the grounds. We clung to each other, scared of being hit by the flying stone, as each massive piece slid into its place. Slowly, we watched the Marble Palace return to its former glory, as it became whole once more.

"That was incredible!" I called to Elva. She didn't respond. Instead, she waved her hand in an all too familiar fashion, and the same silver framed mirror appeared that we had used to return to the Capitol. After a few moments, out stepped the Queen, King, and Prince, as well as Elva's parents and brother.

"Elva!" Evanna cried, flying to her daughter's side, and pulling her close. Elva appeared to crumble in her arms, letting herself melt into her mother, as Ford and Fillipe joined in greeting their daughter and sister. Evanna let her go long enough to hold her face in her hands before she let out a sob and threw her arms back around Elva's neck.

"So, you have completed your task?" Queen Eleria asked, coming to stand beside us, baby Elora in her arms.

"Not quite," I answered. "We still don't have the Heart, and we have a lot to tell you, starting with sending a team to Vincit Omnia Veritas."

She looked shocked at the suggestion but nodded. "We do have much to talk about, don't we? As for the Heart, we shall see what we can do about that," she replied, striding up the stairs.

Elva extracted herself from her family as the Queen met her by the main doors. After a few short words, Elva nodded and walked inside, followed by her family. The Queen gestured for us to follow.

§

The royals were all devastated by the revelation of Ariannah's involvement. Her body had been collected by palace guards and laid in the infirmary, where she remained in an enchanted sleep. The King had not been impressed with Elva's judgement.

"YOU HAD THE OPPORTUNITY TO GET RID OF A MAJOR THREAT TO THE CROWN, THE WOMAN WHO STOLE THE PRINCESS, AND INSTEAD YOU PUT HER TO *SLEEP?*" he had roared angrily.

"My responsibility is to protect Valeria," Elva had responded smoothly. "Not to dictate who lives and who dies."

"No! We do, and you answer to us! She should be executed immediately! What if she wakes and causes further destruction?" he continued to rant. "After all we did for that girl, *she deserves whatever she gets!*"

"I answer to the Heart and the Heart only. As long as she sleeps, she is no longer a threat, and she will remain asleep as long as I see fit," Elva had insisted with a tone of finality, before leaving the King to his rage.

Now, we were in a meeting room on the ground floor. "So; Rogue and Ranger," Elva breathed, sitting across the large blackthorn table from us, hands clasped. "You've come for the Heart of Valeria," she went on. "It won't be easy to convince me to part with it."

"We just saved your life!" Rogue retorted. "Risking our own in the process!"

"And I'll never forget you for it," she answered softly. "I'll never be able to repay you for what you did for me, but the Heart isn't about me. It belongs to Valeria."

Rogue and I looked at each other. Rogue nodded, so we told her a story. We told her of our ancestors, our home, Ventura Estate, the Heart... and the mirrors. "We need the Heart of Valeria; to reconnect it to the others and make it whole again," Rogue finished. "Only then will all of the worlds be safe from Raphael."

We stood there in silence for a while; Elva looking from us to the locket around her neck, which was in the shape of an elf holding a staff. It was still pulsing with a pinkish glow. "Do you know that everything everyone knows about being the Guardian is wrong?" she asked. I looked up at her curiously. "Everyone thinks it's this incredible honour," she smiled sadly. "'what good fortune it is to have been chosen!' they cry. It isn't at all. In fact, it is quite the opposite. The burden is mercilessly draining; and contrary to popular belief, I didn't ask for this."

"What?" I responded, shocked. "I thought the selection process was by application?"

"People only think that because when the first Guardian was killed~" she tilted her head in respect to the Queen, for her uncle.

"~many applied to be the new Guardian. I was chosen, but I never applied."

Only the Queen appeared unfazed by this sudden revelation. "Then how~?" Fillipe began.

"~A compulsion came over me, at what I later learned was the final moment of his life, to travel to his location," Elva continued, looking down at her hands while she played with her fingers; anything to stop herself from looking us in the eyes. "I flew, swam, and walked for days, not stopping for food, water, or sleep.

"When I finally arrived, his body was surrounded by the Heart's pink glow, and the bodies of the attackers he had managed to take down lay scattered on the ground around him. I crossed the barrier and became one with the Heart. The previous Guardian's memories were given to me and I was able to relay what had happened to the Queen," she told us stoically.

She sighed and looked up. "Not a choice. Not good fortune; only a never ending commitment to the Heart and the people of Valeria. This is the responsibility I bear every day, and I do so with unwavering dedication. This is not the life I chose, but the life that chose me. Despite being a piece of something larger, this Heart is here to protect Valeria, and I am here to protect it. The Heart cannot be taken from here, not while there is civil unrest that threatens us all," she finished.

The room was silent. The King was nodding, agreeing with the decision. Ford and Evanna seemed unnerved by their daughter's story, never knowing that she had been forced into Guardianship. Fillipe and Prince Fallon eyed each other off nervously.

The Queen looked unsure of what to do. She looked from Elva to Rogue and me, torn. "We all know the importance of the prophecy and allowing Rogue and Raven to see it to fruition, but my duty to my people is of utmost importance," she paused, looking to the basket on the table in front of her, which held Princess Elora.

"That being said… Rogue and Ranger saved my daughter, and that can't go unacknowledged either, especially when them taking the Heart is for the greater good of our world. While I have no authority over Elva as Guardian, I stand with them in this."

The King looked mutinous. "EVEN IF IT MEANS OUR DOWNFALL?" he exploded in outrage.

The Queen regarded him with cool disdain. "Yes," she answered flatly. "If we, as a royal family, have lost the faith of our people, we are of no use to them," she explained. "If we cannot win our people back; all of our people, then whoever they choose to take over will surely do right by the crown. The people won't accept them otherwise."

"You would just give away the crown, our titles? For what? For the cries of the pixies, sprites, fairies, and every half breed out there complaining that elves believe we're better than they?" the King raged on. "THE VERY IDEA IS OUT-RAGEOUS! WE HAVE A LARGE ENOUGH ARMY! WE COULD WIPE THEM OUT BARELY LIFTING A FING-!"

"-But Husband!" the Queen interrupted his tirade. "With no sprites, fairies, or pixies, who would we rule?"

"Elves!" he yelled back. "And those of the other races who remain loyal, or at least submissive!"

"And how much loss of life would that cost?" the Queen questioned, unruffled by her husband's aggression.

"AS MUCH AS NECESSARY!" he roared, pounding his fist on the table angrily, red in the face.

The Queen paused briefly, before saying quietly: "I agree with you." The King looked confused, then pleased. "The cost of life should be whatever is necessary to secure Valeria."

Elva looked on with interest. Ford and Evanna, who had been silently watching the exchange until now, stood up. Prince Fallon's eyes widened. Fillipe clapped his hand over his mouth.

"You can't be serious?" I broke out. This was not how things were supposed to happen. "Waging a war would devastate Valeria!"

"This is not the place for you to have an opinion!" King Evendon snapped. "You are an outsider-"

"-I am not proposing a war," the Queen interrupted smoothly.

The King deflated somewhat. "B-but you just said-"

"I said," the Queen stated firmly, standing up. "That the cost of life should be whatever is necessary to secure Valeria. As Queen, I am the one that decides what exactly that figure is, and I have decided, that is it zero." The King went red again and started to splutter. "I WILL NOT HAVE MY CHILDREN AT RISK *EVER* AGAIN, AND IF THAT MEANS HANDING OVER THE CROWN, SO BE IT!" Queen Eleria told him fiercely, before taking a breath to calm herself. When she spoke again, her voice was deadly soft. "As Queen, I hereby strip you of your crown and title, Evendon of Eliad."

Evanna gasped, holding one hand to her heart while she fanned herself with the other. Elva raised her eyebrows at the announcement but said nothing. The no-longer-King Evendon, however, started towards the Queen. "You cannot do this!" He reached towards her, hands outstretched.

He got within a finger length's reach before he froze, surrounded by a bright pink glow. "*The Queen, while she remains so, is protected,*" Elva said quietly, but the voice was not hers. Elva's eyes were alight and her voice was smooth and deep.

"Romira?" Rogue whispered. Elva's head turned to her and smiled warmly, not relinquishing her hold on King-no-more Evendon.

"*Not always,*" a third unrecognisable voice replied.

"Please," Queen Eleria begged Elva, her head bowed. "Do not harm him. I want no more bloodshed."

Elva's eyes flashed and the light flickered out, leaving her brilliant blue in their place. "I will place him somewhere he can harm no one but himself," she said, her voice back to normal. She waved her arm and the once King Evendon, disappeared.

"What did he mean?" Rogue asked. "About what you did for Ariannah? How was she involved with you to begin with? She made it clear that she felt she was being used."

Eleria sighed. "In a sense, yes, this was true. Ariannah's father was an incredibly powerful elf. We believe that's why she was so strong, and Evendon believed her powers and her status as an elven sprite hybrid could be used to quell the rebellion.

"She had been selected to marry Fallon so we would appear more tolerant." Her mouth was in a hard line. "I wish I had stepped in and absolved her of such a responsibility sooner. I knew it wasn't what either of them wanted," she admitted shamefully.

"Did you really mean what you said?" I asked Eleria, changing the subject. "That you would just give up your crown without question?"

"Who's to say it was really mine?" she replied, shaking her head. "It was given to me for no other reason than that my mother wished for me to have it. I married so that I could have children and complete the royal family. I had more than one child because I was expected to bear a daughter to take the throne after me." She closed her eyes and took a deep breath before she opened them again, turning to face her son.

"My children are worth far more to me than any title. I have not acted in their best interests, and I will gladly step aside for a leader the public wants if it means guaranteeing their safety." She held her forehead to Prince Fallon's for a moment, before straightening again and picking up her daughter from the basket.

"I am ready. Elva, please send a message throughout Valeria, announcing my abdication and inviting to the Capitol, those who wish to vie for the title."

Elva looked concerned. "Are you sure?"

The Queen was nodding, but I couldn't stay quiet any longer. It was surprising I had managed to as long as I had. "NO!" I cried out. "You can't do this!"

"Ranger~" Rogue started, but I ignored her.

"~Eleria, regardless of how you came to have the crown, you do right by your people! You just threw your husband away for trying to start a war! You're willing to step down to ensure no one gets hurt! You put Valeria first and that's what it needs in a leader!" I ranted.

The Queen clasped her hands together and held them to her mouth. "But the people have lost faith in me. They believe I'm biased and that the other races cannot thrive under an elven leader. What other choice is there?"

After a few moment's silence, Elva stood up and touched the locket. "Ok, I will sen~"

"~WAIT!" Rogue cried. Elva paused; her hands partially raised. "You're an elven leader, but that doesn't mean you necessarily need to lead alone!"

"What do you mean, Rogue?" the Queen pressed. "Having a husband didn't exactly help matters. Are you suggesting I find a suitable marriage among the other races for balance?"

Rogue was waving her hands. "No! No, no, no! That wouldn't work anyway because there are more than two races in Valeria, and the others would still be left feeling unheard and ignored. But~!"

"~But you could invite others to lead with you!" I cut in, finally catching on. Rogue nodded, grinning. "Back home, none of the world leaders do it alone! They have deputies and vice presidents and second in commands and *panels of advisors!*"

"They're specifically there to help the leader make decisions that are best for everyone as a whole, by dividing up territory and finding out what is important to the people within their area and what issues they're having!" I rambled on. The Queen was shaking her head, seemingly confused by the idea, but Elva looked impressed. "Don't you get it? You don't abdicate so a fairy, sprite, or pixie can take over; you invite them to help you rule!"

The Queen looked deep in thought as she considered the idea. "Advisors... We make the decisions together."

Evanna piped up, her hand in the air to get attention. "So members of all races would have a say in rulings for the kingdom?"

"Yes," the Queen confirmed, nodding resolutely. "Together. Elva, summon the heads of all race groups in every city and town in Valeria!" Elva grinned and waved her arm, and once again, the large, silver mirror appeared.

CHAPTER 21

A Fresh Start

§§

"The peoples of Valeria are many and varied, and as such, its leaders must be also!" Queen Eleria was saying from the balcony that overlooked the capital city of Levindra. "Henceforth, a panel of advisors has been convened to ensure the needs of all of Valeria are met! May I present to you, Naevia of the pixies, Glenrock of the sprites, and Evanna of the fairies!"

Naevia appeared as a glowing ball of orange light, but within, Naevia had long limbs, needle like wings, and green spiked hair. Glenrock was a middle aged man with broad shoulders, orange, and black monarch butterfly wings, and a greying beard. Both had been leaders in the rebellion.

"Naevia and Glenrock have both been pivotal in fostering peace between the crown and those who considered its very existence unfair to the people of Valeria! It is my hope, that with them by my side, we will move into a more prosperous time for all!" The Queen's speech was met with riotous cheers.

"Each of your new advisors will have a team within each city, whose job is to ensure the needs of their race are being considered and solutions to their problems; found. I will now leave them to introduce themselves and inform you all of whom to seek out within your cities for guidance! Naevia, if you will!"

The Queen went to step down from the podium when a voice called out from the crowd. "What about your succession? Will the Princess still inherit the throne?"

The Queen paused, holding up a hand to Naevia, who flew back to their place. "No," she answered, before raising her voice. "The idea of inherited leadership is outdated, and only invites corruption! The advisors and I aim to work together as a team, and as such, who makes up that team is highly important. That decision will be left to the people.

"Every five years, those of each race who have dedicated themselves to the betterment of Valeria, will be eligible for participation in the selection process, which will be determined by popular vote. A secondary vote will be held to determine the new, or continuing, reigning monarch, from the four chosen advisors."

Cheers once again erupted from the crowd. "Well, I guess there's no need to wonder who's winning the first election," I nudged Rogue with a wink and a grin, as Naevia returned to the podium.

Elva had stood with us throughout the Queen's speech. When Naevia finished introducing themselves and their city co-advisors, and Glenrock had moved to take the position at the podium, she murmured to us, "I will give you the Heart."

§

The speeches were long over. All over Valeria, meetings were taking place where the chosen city or town officials were discussing the new decisions made by the Queen, and what the advisory panel meant for everyone. As the Elven Advisor to the Observatory, Elva's father, Ford, had returned to convene his meeting, while her mother, Evanna, now Fairy Advisor to the Crown, was travelling from city to city, town to town, introducing herself and her fairy officials to their constituents. Queen Eleria, now the Elven Advisor to the Crown also, had left for Farivian, to assign Jahra to the position of Elven Advisor to the city.

"I've never felt the power of the Heart so strongly before you came here," Elva was saying, shivering slightly. "I feel as though that is a sign." Slowly, Elva took the locket from around her neck and passed it to me. The second she had, a cold chill settled on us.

"To be bound to the Heart for so long… This is how it feels to be parted from it," she whispered, paling slightly "I can't say I enjoy the feeling."

"Neither do I," Rogue agreed, her arms around herself. "It's so cold."

We had been analysing the mirror riddle, trying to figure out where we'd find the next one. "Tell me again?" I asked Rogue, trying to ignore the cold.

"*The second can be found where all is cleansed, this task, you will find, is draining; fit for a Queen, it is larger than the rest, you mustn't keep the merfolk waiting,*" she repeated for the twelfth time. We'd brought the Castle of Ventura blueprints with us, as well as the map of the castle grounds, and the riddle that would lead us to each of the seven mirrors.

"Merfolk?" Elva said. "I remember them."

"You do?" Rogue asked. "How? Do you have them here?"

"No," she smiled, shaking her head. "I've seen Romira creating them… in the memories of the Heart." She gazed at the necklace, now around my neck.

"Well, the first mirror; the one that led us here; was found in the sunroom. You can easily see the clues to where it's hidden in the riddle," Rogue explained, pushing the scroll across the table so Elva could read it.

"Was it easy to find?" Elva questioned.

"Well," I winced. "We tore apart one of the other rooms in the attempt… but we got it eventually!" We all laughed, but I felt a stab of pain in my heart to think about home, and worried for the people we'd left behind.

"'Where all is cleansed'… Could it mean the kitchen?" she put in helpfully, leaning over to see the castle blueprints.

"It's possible," I nodded.

"Yes! Stained dishes become clean again in the kitchen!" Rogue jumped in. "And the riddle says the task is draining! Nothing is more draining than dishes!"

I frowned. "A seven foot high and five foot wide mirror isn't going to fit in a sink, let alone down the plug hole!"

"What about the bathhouse?" Elva suggested, before checking the castle maps. "I mean the bath…room. You cleanse bodies there?"

"That'd be right!" Rogue burst out. "The castle has six of them! It'll take forever to search all of them, and they all have big mirrors!"

All was silent as Elva studied the blueprints and Rogue read the riddle. "What's it like in your world?" she asked us softly after a period of silence.

"Nothing like this. There's a lot more emphasis on nature and magic here," I replied. "People don't love nature so much that it loves them back," I told her, thinking about the Farivian maples.

"I wish I could see it," she whispered. She was quiet for a short time. She seemed to be considering something. "If I'm not the Guardian anymore… can I go home?" Elva asked suddenly.

I paused. "I don't know. I guess so? What other options are there?"

"Well…" she started slowly, a thoughtful look crossing her face. "I could… come with you."

"What?" Rogue exclaimed.

"Think about it," she answered, her face deadly serious. "This doesn't feel right. I can still feel the Heart reaching out to me. Whether by choice or not, I am the Guardian. For all you know you need me as much as you need the Heart! And surely the more help you have, the easier this task will be!"

Rogue and I deliberately avoided her eyes, glancing at each other uneasily. She wasn't wrong. I could feel the Heart calling; but could we put her at risk to have her join us? Surely people from the Venturan worlds weren't meant to be brought into ours. It would be too dangerous. We'd risk exposure. More importantly, what if she didn't survive?

What if none of us do? A deep voice cut into my thoughts. Rogue gasped. Elva closed her eyes and sighed deeply.

Romira?

Yes, my child. A Heart in pieces is a Heart in turmoil. Raven could not have predicted what a torn Heart would feel or need. The Guardian provided a warm soul for me to heal within. As such, the Guardians are bonded to me. It is not possible to separate us now. We are one.

I took the locket from my neck and instantly, began to feel better. Until then, I hadn't noticed the weight it had placed on me. The moment I handed it back to Elva, I breathed deeply with relief. Both Rogue and I could feel the Heart sigh as it connected with Elva's neck.

"That is better," Elva and Romira said together.

"So," Elva continued alone, looking from Rogue to me and back again. "Is it decided?"

I shook my head and shrugged, looking at Rogue, who looked likewise flabbergasted at the turn of events. "Why not?" I said finally.

CHAPTER 22

Goodbye

§§

"You're leaving?" Evanna cried, sobbing into her husband's arms. The news had not been received well. "But you just came home!"

"Mother, I would need to leave anyway," Elva explained gently. "If I were to stay, I'd need to go back into hiding, except without the Heart, I'd have nothing to defend myself."

"We could protect you," Ford answered grimly, his hands tightening around his wife. The Queen watched the exchange, remaining uninvolved, her daughter on her hip, her son by her side.

"Father, I love you, but it's not your job to protect me anymore; your responsibility is to the elves of the Observatory, and mine is to the Heart… wherever it goes," she told him.

Her mother quietened but didn't stop entirely. Fillipe just stood next to them, looking uncomfortable. "So you're just leaving the world… like you're dying?"

"No!" Elva laughed, hugging her brother. "It is not dying." She turned to us quickly. "Right?"

"No," I confirmed. "Unless crossing through the mirror the first time was, in fact, us dying and this is the afterlife." Ford looked angry as Evanna started to cry again, so I stopped talking.

"You'll miss my wedding," Fillipe said softly, tears in his eyes.

"I know!" Elva cried out, hugging him again. "I read in your letter that you and Fallon had finally announced your engagement and I couldn't be happier for you!" She held her brother's hands. "This is for everyone. You can't live a happy life here together if there's no world to live in."

"All is as it should be, Mother!" Prince Fallon told Evanna affectionately. "Including!" he continued, turning to Elva. "My future sister in law joining Rogue and Ranger on their quest."

"I will be fine," Elva promised her family, smiling. "And we could still have plenty of time together. We can't leave until we know where the next mirror is, and even then, we don't know how to get back."

"What mirror do you speak of?" Queen Eleria asked earnestly.

"We came here through a mirror," Rogue reminded her. "We need to find a mirror to take us back, and we need to find the mirror leading to Romira's next world before we do."

"Why can't you look for it once you're there?" Prince Fallon asked.

"We can," I answered. "It'll just be safer if we already have a solid idea of where we're going first. Raphael has almost caught us twice already."

"Raphael is still alive?" the Queen exclaimed, holding her daughter close.

"We don't think so," Rogue told her, shaking her head. "He doesn't have a body or anything, but something about him is still in the castle, trying to get to the Hearts."

"You think it wise taking one directly to him?" Ford challenged.

"Hush, Father," Elva snapped. "I won't let anything happen to the Heart. If he's as weakened as Rogue and Ranger say, then the power of the Heart will be enough to get past him and to the second mirror."

"Once we know where it is," Rogue cut in.

"Ooooonce we know where it is," I sighed in agreement.

"What did the riddle say?" the Queen asked. We repeated it for her.

"We figured out it was more than likely one of the bathrooms, but there's a lot of them and there's no way of knowing which one it is," Rogue explained.

"Well… your riddle says it's fit for a Queen, does it not?" she smiled coyly. "Follow me." We followed her up a high sweeping staircase, to the upper floors of the Marble Palace.

On our way, we passed workers of all kinds, dutifully preparing quarters within the palace for all of the Crown Advisors and city officials. They were to be welcomed at the palace whenever they visited the Capitol, as equals.

The Queen finally stopped by a wide, semicircular archway. It had no doors, but a watery veil obscured the room beyond. "Welcome to my private bathhouse," she announced, stepping through the veil.

It was glorious. Sun shone down from a huge opening in the ceiling. It was a skylight without the glass, another magical barrier protecting it from the elements. The bath itself was as large as a swimming pool, with all manner of bottles lined up along the edge. Several mirrors of different shapes and sizes hung on the walls above a large dressing table, covered in powders, brushes, and perfume bottles.

"Fit for a Queen," I whispered, staring at the bath.

"What?" Rogue questioned.

"What does that remind you of?" I asked her, pointing. "The golden taps, the square shape, the size?"

"All but one bathroom has a bath," Elva said, having pulled out the blueprints.

"Yes," Rogue nodded in agreement. "But only one has a bath anywhere near that size."

"So if we know where we're going, how do we get back to Ventura?" Elva asked.

"I don't know!" I answered helplessly. "Valeria is safe, isn't it? Do we have to find a mirror here too?" I turned to

Elva and shook her slightly. "Romira! Are you in there? Help us!"

"Ranger! St~!" Elva started to squeal, but stopped mid-sentence, as Romira's voice replaced hers. "*The pages,*" he whispered.

"Pages?" Rogue repeated. "What pages?"

"The pages!" Elva gasped, returning to herself. She stepped back and spread her arms, clapping her hands together at her chest as we'd seen her do before. The necklace glowed brightly before a yellowing envelope appeared in front of her. It was clearly hundreds of years old. She handed it to Rogue, who gave it to me. It felt like it would crumble in my hands as I opened it and pulled out the mysterious 'pages'.

"What is this?" Rogue asked Elva, starting to read over my shoulder.

"A message," Elva responded quietly. "Left in the first Guardian's care soon after he was given the Heart."

I looked down and began to read aloud:

To the Queen of Valeria,

No doubt, I am long dead, but there is still work to be done. I am heartbroken to learn that my son, Raphael, is seeking the worlds of Ventura for himself. Had Raven not come to me, I would never have known.

With the castle of Ventura's third floor only just finished, I fear I may not live to see its completion. Hope is still alive, for I do have a plan.

My heart and soul has been devoted to creating seven worlds and when I am gone, they will be alone, with no protection. With my death close at hand, I will use what remains of my strength to extract my own heart and give it to the castle of Ventura. With my Heart within the castle, the energy and love I placed into the creation of the worlds will protect them. My only hope remains with this plan, for with its failure, comes the seven Venturan world's destruction.

I tell you this, for I have told my daughter, Raven, of my plan. She tells me she has visions of two young girls, descendants to us both, who are to rid the Venturan worlds of Raphael's danger for good. Should she, or these girls, ever come to you with a warning, I beg you heed them. I warn you, for should Raphael ever find a way to take over, Valeria is the first world of the seven. Please take precautions... for your future.

My time nears...

Romira

"He didn't know that Raven was going to split the Heart," Rogue breathed softly.

"How could he have?" I asked her. "It wasn't until he had died that she did it. Raphael realised he couldn't get into the worlds, then figured out why. It was only then that he tried to find the Heart, so he could get in."

"Then Raven stole the Heart before he could, split it into pieces, and travelled to each of the seven worlds," Rogue went on.

I looked to the next page and found a slightly newer piece of paper. This one was from Raven.

I write this in haste.

I have delivered the first piece of the Heart to the world of Valeria's Guardian. I fear that one small piece will not be enough to fight Raphael off. I pray the Heart of my dear departed father will make the piece sufficient to protect the people. Once I have left, he will gain access to this World.

I need to move quickly. I fear I will not be fast enough to reach every world in time. This message lies in wait for Rogue and Ranger, who are the only two with the power to reunite the Heart when the time comes. Only they, with the Heart, can rid Ventura of Raphael's malice and hatred.

I will leave a message in each world. If you are reading this now, I pray you to hasten to Mattara as soon as possible. Once in Valeria, Raphael will know and try to follow you. You will have very little time before he will be able to breach the boundary; ESPECIALLY once you have the Heart. Be on the lookout for anything strange and remember to stick together. When in the Venturan worlds, you are your only weapon.

Raven.

"This was left with it," the Queen whispered, giving me a glass box. "When Raven left the letter, it was inside."

When I opened it, I felt a strange emptiness and realised what it was. "It's the original case that held the Heart of Ventura," I gasped. Rogue touched the lid reverently. The necklace around Elva's neck began to pulse... and the full length mirror hanging on the wall began to shimmer. We all looked to it in amazement, Ford moving forward to examine the glowing frame.

"Looks like it's time to go," Rogue whispered. She looked at Elva. "Are you sure you're ready to do this?"

"Yes," she sighed, taking a shuddering breath. "This is right. The Heart is meant to be with me... but it needs to go with you too." She turned to her parents. "I need to go with them. I know I've only just gotten back, but this has to happen." Evanna looked on the verge of screaming, but Ford's face had softened.

Fillipe grinned. "Go for it!" he nodded, jumping forward to hug her one last time.

"W-we lo-love y-you, Honey," her mother sobbed.

Elva hugged her parents tightly, then turned to us, her face glowing slightly in the setting sun bearing down through the skylight. "I'm ready," she said. She joined Rogue and me as we walked towards the shimmering mirror, sitting on the wall in its glossy cedar frame.

I turned back to the Queen. "Good luck," I breathed. She smiled back.

Rogue, Elva, and I nodded to each other before I took a step forward and melted into the glass.